NIGHTMARE ACADEMY
MONSTER WAR

5TH RING

4TH RING

3RD RING

2ND RING

1ST RING

SECRETS OF THE NETHER

KNOWN GREMLIN
INFESTATION

HAGS OF
THE VOID

TROUT OF TRUTH

NETHERFORGE

HYDRA CAVE
(RUMOURED)

BT GRAVEYARD

INNER CIRCLE

First
published
in paperback in
Great Britain by
HarperCollins *Children's Books* 2009
HarperCollins *Children's Books* is a division of
HarperCollins*Publishers* Ltd
77-85 Fulham Palace Road, Hammersmith, London W6
8JB

The HarperCollins website address is:

www.harpercollins.co.uk

1

Text copyright © Dean Lorey 2009
Illustrations © Brandon Dorman 2009

ISBN 978-0-00-725721-8

Dean Lorey and Brandon Dorman assert the moral right
to be identified as the author and illustrator of the work.

Printed and bound in England by Clays Ltd, St Ives plc

NIGHTMARE ACADEMY
MONSTER WAR

DEAN LOREY

For more ferocious monster fun log on to
www.nightmareacademy.co.uk

HarperCollins *Children's Books*

To three people who helped and encouraged me

when it meant the most:

Dr Jean Fant

Tim Schoch

And, most of all, Francesca Rizzo

PART ONE
ATTACK OF THE FIFTH

CHAPTER ONE
THE WAR
BEGINS

L ike most big and terrible things, the war between the people of Earth and the monsters of the Nether started out small.

At first, there were just a few isolated attacks. A group of hikers in Maui were set upon by a pack of Dangeroos. The filthy, kangaroo-like beasts stuffed the screaming humans into their pouches and then hopped off into the dense and humid jungle beyond.

The hikers were never seen again.

Several postal workers in the small town of Conyers, Georgia were bitten by one-eyed serpents that lay coiled in mailboxes. The shiny purple beasts came to be known as Yeller-Swellers because their bite caused people to yell loudly in pain and then swell up like giant marshmallows. Fortunately, the swelling was only temporary. Unfortunately, when the victims shrank back down, they didn't *stop* shrinking until they were half their original size.

Even the President of the United States was a victim of Monster Attack.

Although he had some of the best security of anyone on the planet, nothing could protect him from his own nightmares. While sleeping in the presidential suite in the White House, he dreamed that he was walking through his old school completely naked. In the dream, everyone pointed at him and laughed – his teachers, his parents and even his dog, Herbert. In fact, Herbert's laughter was so cruel and mean-spirited that it caused the President to have a panic attack and, quite unconsciously, he opened a fiery purple portal to the Netherworld.

A Mimic slithered through.

Using its long arms and fingers, it quickly abducted the man, stashed him in a cupboard and then changed form to 'mimic' him so precisely that even the President's wife couldn't tell the difference, although she *did* mention that he smelled strongly of cinnamon –a common trait of Mimics.

That afternoon, the thing that looked like the President held a press conference. In front of the entire world, it began rhyming like an insane Dr Seuss, telling everyone that the "Monsters are *why*, we're all gonna *die* – so let's just eat *pie*. Good*bye*!" Then the creature did backflips through the astonished throng of reporters until its true identity was revealed when it knocked over a water bottle and the resulting splash of liquid caused its skin to melt away like candle wax.

After the monster was captured and destroyed, the real President was rescued. The shaken man wasted no time before holding another press conference to explain to the world that no one should panic and that things were completely under control.

But they weren't.

Sitting in his parents' apartment in Brooklyn, Charlie Benjamin watched TV with growing anxiety as CNN showed endless reports of Nethercreatures rampaging through cities around the globe. Flocks of Hags spiralled out of a night-time sky to snatch entire football teams from their stadiums – the starting line-up of the Dallas Cowboys was the most recent casualty. Gremlins gorged themselves on power cables at plants throughout the world, plunging entire cities into darkness. In fact, Tokyo was just recovering from a Gremlin-caused blackout.

The fear brought on by these attacks caused millions of nightmares in people across the planet. In turn, those nightmares opened portals to the Netherworld, allowing an incredible influx of new monsters to pour through. Charlie had been taught in his 'Monster Invasion: What You Can Do About It' class that this was called the 'Snowball Effect'. But to learn about it in a schoolroom was one thing – seeing it in action was something terrifyingly different.

"Horrible, horrible…" Charlie's father Barrington muttered as he watched the attacks unfold.

"Yes, indeed," his wife Olga agreed. She smoothed her dress and sighed heavily. "Why are they doing this to us, Charlie?"

"Because they can."

He knew the answer wasn't very satisfying, but it was *true*. The monsters were attacking because it was in their nature to attack – it was simply what they were born to do, and they were doing it now with terrifying gusto.

And all because of me, Charlie thought glumly, although he didn't say it.

The attack of the monsters of the Nether wasn't his fault, not really, but he'd certainly contributed to their getting to Earth in the first place.

For six months, he and his friends had studied Banishing and Nethermancy at the Nightmare Academy, honing their skills in preparation to one day go to work for the Nightmare Division – the organisation charged with controlling the Nethercreature population on Earth. During their final exam, they stumbled across a plot to bring the last two Named Lords of the Nether out of that terrible land of monsters and here to our world.

Despite Charlie's best efforts (or maybe *because* of them, depending on who you talked to) the Named succeeded in their evil scheme and managed to summon the Fifth – a creature of unimaginable power. She promptly destroyed all the Named Lords and established herself as the General of the Army of the Nether, sending her ferocious minions out across the planet to wreak havoc on humanity.

Someone had to take the blame, and Director Drake of the Nightmare Division blamed Charlie and sent him into exile.

As much as he was desperate to leave his parents' apartment and return to his friends at the Nightmare Academy, Charlie didn't see how he could. If he left his mum and dad alone, they would most likely be monster food within minutes. Plus, there was that sticky matter of his being 'exiled'. He didn't know what it *meant* exactly, but he suspected it involved him being banished from the Academy – maybe for ever.

Not that a little thing like 'banishment' was going to stop him. As far as Charlie was concerned, nothing was going to prevent him from seeing Violet, Theodore and Brooke again after he was sure his parents were safe from the monsters of the Nether. And then… something miraculous happened.

The monsters gave up.

As quickly as the attacks on humanity had started, they stopped. For a full week, there were no monster sightings anywhere on planet Earth. Across the globe, people celebrated and rejoiced. They even went back to their old routines, sure that the Monster War was finally over.

"Charlie, you're too thin," his mother scolded as he nibbled at his burger. Charlie kept glancing at the door of the restaurant, sure that some horrible beast was going to lurch in – but the place remained calm and quiet.

"I'm fine, Mom. Really."

"There's nothing wrong with him," his father said, gulping down a chocolate milkshake. "The boy is just growing taller. Children are like toffee – as you stretch them, they get thinner."

"Well, I think it's stress. For almost a year now, he's been expected to save the entire world from monsters all on his own. I mean, he hasn't even kissed a girl yet."

"Mom!"

"Well, it's true."

Not really, Charlie thought, thinking of the quick kiss he'd shared with Brooke on the beach in front of the Nightmare Academy six months ago, but he didn't say anything. He glanced again at the front door.

"Will you please stop doing that?" Olga snapped. "Nothing is coming through there! Goodness gracious – no one has seen a monster in over a week."

"Yeah, but that doesn't mean they're not around... hiding... waiting to attack."

"And why is that your problem?" His mother angrily jabbed a French fry into her ketchup. "Let the adults in the Nightmare Division handle it – you're still a child! *My* child! And as long as you're with us, we will protect *you* – not the other way around. That's just the way it works in the real world."

Yeah, right, Charlie thought. The image of his parents protecting him from monsters was so laughable that he couldn't even conjure it up.

"Well, we may be the adults," his father said, "but the fact remains that Charlie is an extraordinarily good monster hunter. He's a... what do they call you?"

"A Double-Threat."

"Double-Threat! Yes, indeed! The boy can both Banish and Nethermance – most children can't do *either*."

"Well, he didn't ask for this horrible ability," his mother replied icily. "I'm just thankful the monsters have stopped attacking so we can stop worrying about it."

Charlie shook his head. "It's not over."

"How do you *know*?"

"I just do. I can... I can feel it. Something is coming, something *bad* and I've got to..." He hesitated. *"I've got to leave you and go and find my friends at the Academy – I've got to get ready to fight"* were the words he knew he *should* say – but the panicked, desperate look in his mother's eyes stopped him.

"Charlie Benjamin," she said with a sigh. "You know I love you more than life itself... but you can't possibly get rid of all the monsters in the world."

And that was when a Netherbat crashed through the large front window of the restaurant.

I may not be able to get rid of all the monsters in the world, Charlie thought as the crimson beast sailed inside with a shriek, furiously flapping its leathery wings as startled customers dived for cover from the terrible spray of glass, *but I can get rid of* this *one*.

He reached under the table and drew his glowing blue rapier – it felt good in his hand. With another ear-piercing shriek, the Netherbat snatched a screaming, stocky man in its talons, then spun around and flapped towards the broken window, trying to escape with its flailing prize.

Charlie leaped into the air and, with one quick, smooth move, brought his sizzling rapier down on the beast's left wing. The Netherbat fell to the ground in a fountain of black ichor and, off balance now, careened into a table in a gloopy explosion of mustard and ketchup. Still flapping with its one remaining wing, it flipped on to its back and slammed into the restaurant wall. The nearby customers scrambled to crawl away as the beast snapped at them – until Charlie put a quick stop to that by chopping off the Netherbat's head.

"Th-thank you!" the stocky man exclaimed as Charlie yanked him from the dead creature's spasming talons. But before Charlie could mutter "You're welcome", two more monstrous bats sailed in, searching for tasty human prey. Charlie gutted one of the beasts as it soared above him and then quickly dispatched the other as it flew into the kitchen. The creature's carcass slammed down on to the grill, where it cooked and sizzled alongside the burgers and fried onions.

There was silence then, broken only by the popping of frying meat. After a moment, it was joined by another sound.

Clapping.

Charlie turned to see the customers in the restaurant applauding as they struggled to their feet. "Oh, it was nothing," he said, turning a bright shade of red, secretly pleased. But then he heard screaming. A great crowd of people were rushing out of the nearby shopping centre. Something was inside.

Something *bad*.

"Don't," his mother pleaded.

"I have to," Charlie replied and, without another word, he ran out of the restaurant and towards the monsters in the mall.

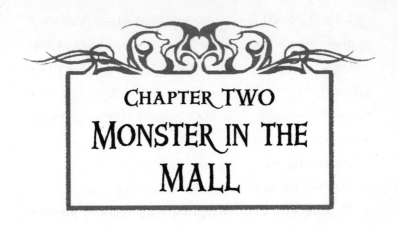

CHAPTER TWO
MONSTER IN THE MALL

Screaming customers flooded from the entrance in waves, and pushing through them was like trying to break through heavy surf. Somehow Charlie managed. Once inside, he tried to distance himself from the cries of the panicked people to figure out the *cause* of their terror. His first clue came from a woman just outside a clothes shop. People streamed past her – mothers clutching children, elderly people hopping along on sticks – but for some reason this woman wasn't moving.

That's strange, Charlie thought. And then he realised *why*.

She was covered, from the neck down, in a clear, gummy mass that completely immobilised her, anchoring her to the floor. Charlie glanced around and saw that she wasn't the only one encased in the gluey mess. A security guard in the food court on the second storey was trapped against the cash register of a Chinese restaurant and two children in the play area were stuck to a giant foam ladybird.

Only one monster does that, Charlie thought. And then he saw it.

A Ravenous Sticky-Spitter.

The large, lizard-like creature clung to the outside of a glass elevator that was making its way back to the first floor. The beast was incredibly hard to spot – Sticky-Spitters had terrific camouflage; the pigment in their skin mirrored their surroundings so perfectly that most people could only see them when they moved. Charlie didn't think he'd ever come into contact with a Sticky-Spitter before, but that didn't mean he hadn't. Before his training at the Nightmare Academy, one could have been sleeping right next to him without him ever seeing it.

As the elevator landed on the first floor, the Sticky-Spitter opened its wide mouth and spat out a large wad of glistening goop that shot through the air and snagged a fleeing shoe-shop assistant.

At least his face isn't covered, Charlie thought, before remembering that Ravenous Sticky-Spitters (or RSSs) preferred to swallow their food alive, so they carefully aimed their spit to immobilise prey, not suffocate it.

With his rapier glowing fiercely blue, Charlie rushed towards the RSS, intent on putting an end to its attacks before feeding time could begin. But as fast as Charlie was, he wasn't faster than the gluey phlegm that the RSS hurled his way, sticking him to the floor like a fly to flypaper. His arms were pinned to his sides and his face was spattered with flecks of glistening spittle – they had the sour smell of a burp that had been fermenting inside a belly for far too long.

OK, Charlie thought calmly, *if I can't Banish it, I'll just Nethermance it away.*

As one of only three people in existence who could both Banish and Nethermance (although not at the same time), Charlie had options available to him that most people with the Gift could only dream of. He had just begun to open a portal beneath the creature when several Netherstalkers suddenly burst through the air shaft in the ceiling above him, quickly descending on long strands of spider-silk. The double eyestalks that waved on their heads told him they were only Class-2 creatures, which wouldn't normally present a problem – but this situation was far from normal.

Normally, Charlie wasn't trapped in a glob of Sticky-Spitter phlegm.

How am I going to get out of this one? he wondered as their large, spidery bodies arrowed down towards him, sharp fangs snapping.

Just before the first of the Netherstalkers pounced on his head, Charlie noticed his father running out of a sports shop, wielding a large baseball bat.

"Get away from my boy!" the tall man shouted. With one mighty swing, he knocked the nearest Netherstalker away. It made a crunching sound, like a snail being crushed underfoot, then swung wildly into the air, still tethered to the thick silken line that spun out of its abdomen.

"Thanks, Dad!" Charlie shouted.

"No time to talk, son," Barrington replied as he swung at another of the descending creatures. Again there was that peculiar crunching sound and the Netherstalker soared away with a squeal. "You may have noticed," Barrington continued, eyeing another of the approaching beasts, "that I've chosen to use a baseball bat made of wood. Why not aluminum, you ask? Because aluminum doesn't compare to the feel of a solid length of northern white ash, that's why."

He shot Charlie a friendly wink just as the hairy bristles on the leg of another Netherstalker landed on Charlie's shoulder. Barrington prepared to swing as Olga rushed up with a can of insect spray.

"Get off him, you filthy bug!" she yelled, spraying the creature right in its waving eyestalks. The Netherstalker shrieked and crashed to the slippery floor.

"Olga Benjamin!" Barrington roared. "Excellent work! Where did you get the bug spray?"

"The chemist's," she replied. "Best thing to get rid of bugs, don't you think?"

Barrington smiled fondly. "My girl…"

The two of them went to work dispatching the rest of the Netherstalkers so that Charlie could go after the Ravenous Sticky-Spitter, which was now moving rapidly towards them. Because its skin was camouflaged so perfectly against the wall of the mall, Charlie had trouble judging exactly how far away it really was.

If he opened a portal behind it, there wouldn't be enough time to open another and the monster would get them and eat them. If he opened a portal too far in front of it, the monster would have time to swerve around the trap and *still* get them and eat them. But if he opened the portal *just right*, directly beneath the rampaging creature, then maybe—

Purple fire blazed across Charlie as a wide portal snapped open right below the fearsome beast. The RSS let out a wail of surprise and then plummeted through the portal and into the Nether, tumbling wildly through the air before crashing into the icy waters of the 4th Ring, where it was consumed by a passing Hydra. Charlie quickly closed the portal and was pleasantly surprised to discover that the purple flame on his body had melted the thick gum of the Sticky-Spitter, freeing him. With a couple swipes of his rapier, he killed the few remaining Netherstalkers, then turned to his parents with a smile.

"You two are… you're Leet!"

Barrington grinned. "I have no idea what that means, but I'll take it as a good thing."

"It is. Trust me."

Olga smiled primly. "I'd better get to work helping out the other unfortunates that have got caught in the big lizard's spit. I'll be in the supermarket getting peanut butter. It helps remove chewing gum from hair, so I don't see why it wouldn't be useful in this situation." With that, she strode off.

"Terrific, isn't she?" Barrington said proudly once Olga was out of earshot.

"Yeah. She really is."

And that's when they heard a scream.

What now? Charlie thought as he and his father raced in the direction of the sound.

The screaming woman stood in front of an electrical

store, pointing at a widescreen TV in the window. Charlie pushed his way through the crowd of people around her to see an aerial view of Central Park in Manhattan – or what Charlie knew *should* have been Central Park. But the wide lawn of Sheep Meadow and the rippling waves of the toy-boat pond were now gone from view, covered by a thick, impenetrable white mist that had settled over the place like an Otherworldly shroud.

"What *is* that weird fog?" a small boy asked, awestruck.

"And where did it come from?" an older man in a baseball cap added.

Charlie thought those were both perfectly legitimate questions, but he had another more urgent one: *what is it hiding?*

Olga Benjamin's peanut-butter idea didn't help free the captured shoppers from the Sticky-Spitter's slime balls, but it turned out that vinegar did – also her idea. After she had finished helping the last of the victims escape their gluey prisons, she met up again with Charlie and Barrington. They were waiting for her in the mall car park, keeping a careful watch on the sky.

"See any Hags?" Olga asked as she walked up.

Charlie shook his head, amused that his mother knew that if they were looking up, they might be searching for Hags. "It looks clear."

"That's good news." Olga smoothed out her dress, which was spotted with monster goop, then turned to Barrington. "It appears that things are finally under control. Ready to head home?"

Barrington nodded. "I am…" He seemed hesitant.

"But?"

"But Charlie has something to tell you."

Olga turned to her son. "Go ahead, Charlie. Don't be shy."

He took a deep breath. "I'm sorry, Mom, but I can't go with you. The monsters are going to keep attacking us – until they're all dead or we are. I just… I need to do what I can to help."

"Of course you do," his mother replied promptly.

Charlie wasn't sure he'd heard correctly. Where was the explosion of dismay? The pleading that he come to his senses and return home, where it was safe?

"You have a destiny," his mother said, cradling his cheeks in her warm hands. "I didn't want to acknowledge it before, but now that I've seen how skilfully you handle yourself and how much good you can do for others, I can't deny it." She smiled gently.

"You go on and do what you need to, son."

"I wish I could stay here and protect you."

Olga shook her head. "Your father and I will be fine." Having just seen them in action, Charlie knew it was true. He hugged her then and she whispered, "Be *safe*." He could feel her breath tickling his ear.

"I will," Charlie promised. Then he turned to his father and extended his hand.

Barrington laughed. "A handshake? You've got to be kidding me!" He snatched his son up in his arms. Charlie could feel his father's stubble on his cheek and he smelled his aftershave. "You go get 'em, son. Then you come back to us, safe and sound, you hear?"

Charlie nodded, then stepped back and opened a portal. The war with the creatures of the Nether had taken a new and unexpected turn and Central Park – with its monstrous mystery – was clearly going to be the next battleground. The real fight was about to begin, and for that Charlie Benjamin needed his friends.

He had to return to the Nightmare Academy.

Charlie waved goodbye to his parents, then jumped through the fiery gateway and was soon gone from view.

CHAPTER THREE
NO PLACE LIKE HOME

Theodore Dagget and Violet Sweet were repainting the outside of the broken yacht that housed the Addy students at the Nightmare Academy when they heard a familiar voice.

"Thought I'd find you painting," Charlie said cheerfully as he walked towards them over the rope bridge that was strung between two huge branches of the mighty banyan tree.

"Charlie!" Violet squealed, running over to him. She hugged him tightly – then quickly drew back.

"What's wrong?" Charlie asked, surprised.

"You shouldn't be here. You're *exiled*. What if someone from the Nightmare Division sees you? It's not safe."

Charlie shrugged. "Nowhere's safe right now – not with all those monsters out there. I'm not going to hide;

I'm going to fight. Besides, no one's keeping me from my best friends – *no one* – not even the Nightmare Division."

Violet burst into a sunny smile and hugged him again, more tightly this time.

"Geez, calm down," Theodore said with a grin, "or you'll knock him off the bridge before he has a chance to save the world."

Charlie laughed. "Yeah, right..." He gestured to Theodore's clothes, which were covered in blue paint. "You get any on the ship or just yourself?"

"Hey, don't give me any grief, OK? I'm a precision instrument! A finely crafted tool for Banishing! Painting is beneath me."

"Yeah, beneath you, above you, in your hair, on your clothes – you've got paint everywhere but where it's supposed to be." Charlie inspected the Addy yacht. There was fresh wood on one side – it looked like it had been recently repaired. "Is that damage from Slagguron?"

Violet nodded. "We've been doing our best to fix things up, but there's still a long way to go."

Just a few weeks earlier, Slagguron, one of the four Named Lords of the Nether, had slammed his wormlike body against the trunk of the massive tree, knocking several boats from its branches and damaging many more. Charlie still found it hard to believe that the raging colossus was dead now – he and all the Named – killed, in an instant, by the Fifth.

"You're thinking about the Fifth, aren't you?" Theodore asked. Charlie always found it eerie how good his best friend was at reading his mind. He nodded.

"Yeah. I guess so."

"Well, stop it! You don't have to kill the most deadly monster the world has ever known right this second. Heck, you can relax for five or ten minutes before you go after her…"

"How generous," Charlie grinned. But his grin quickly faded. "Look, I know I'm not supposed to be here right now – being exiled and all – but I think the Fifth is up to something, something big, and we need to check it out." But before he could continue, a new voice suddenly cried out.

"Charlie Benjamin!"

Charlie turned to see Brooke Brighton waving to him from a platform high above. Even from this far away, he was amazed by how pretty she was.

"Hey, Brooke!"

"Stay right there."

With an excited *whoop!* she slid down a vine strung between her platform and the Addy yacht far below, her long, blonde hair whipping freely in the wind. She landed next to Charlie with the nimbleness of a cat. "I missed you!" she said, then hugged him tightly before giving him a quick, friendly kiss.

There, Charlie thought, remembering his mother telling him he'd never even kissed a girl. *Now I've been kissed twice.*

"Hi, Brooke," Theodore said expectantly. "You miss me too?"

"Lame," Violet said, pretending to cough.

"I am not lame!"

"I didn't say anything. Just had a little tickle in my throat." Violet coughed again and said, "Desperate."

"Hey!"

"Of course I've missed you, silly," Brooke said with a smile. She gave Theodore a quick hug, then turned to Charlie. "So where have you been? Tell us *everything*."

"I will... but you go first. Has anyone from the Nightmare Division been to the Academy?"

Brooke nodded. "Yeah. They checked out the damage that Slagguron did and said they were going to come up with a plan to protect the place. We're completely exposed to the monsters of the Nether now that the Guardian's dead."

The Guardian.

A pang of sadness hit Charlie upon hearing the name

of the small, sad creature whose aura had always protected the Academy from Nethercreatures. Its shocking death had set into motion the horrific chain of events that was still unfolding.

"I still think about him, you know," Charlie said. "How needy he was. He just wanted a friend really."

Violet nodded. "Ever since his death, the Nightmare Division has wanted to station some Banishers and Nethermancers here to protect us."

And to keep me away, Charlie thought. Even though he didn't exactly know the terms of his exile, he knew they wouldn't want him anywhere near the Academy.

"So why did you come here, DT?" Theodore asked. "Is it about what's going on in Central Park?"

Once again, Charlie found it freaky how easily Theodore could read his mind. He nodded. "What do you know about it?"

"Well, what *I* heard," Brooke said, "is that, apparently, the Division used some kind of X-ray equipment to look into the mist."

"And there's things in there!" Theodore exclaimed. "Gross, snail-like creatures. And something else too. Something big is growing in the fog. Something *giant*."

Something giant growing in the fog. That didn't sound good.

"Someone needs to check it out," Charlie said. "And I figure that someone is us. Who's with me?"

But before they could answer, a familiar voice rang out.

"What are y'all yappin' about?"

"Mama Rose!" Charlie yelled as the Housemistress of the Nightmare Academy stepped into view. "Great to see you!"

"I wish I could say the same," the large woman sniffed, her meaty hands on her thick hips. "You're skin and bones, Charlie Benjamin! Now follow me so we can get some grub into you pronto."

Before Charlie could resist, Mama Rose roughly ushered them up to the pirate ship at the very top of the Academy – ever since Slagguron's attack had destroyed the galley, the students had been using it as their new mess hall. Steaming piles of pancakes were heaped in towering stacks on a great wooden table.

"Pancakes for dinner?" Charlie asked with a grin.

"And why not?" Mama Rose replied, her southern accent as thick as the maple syrup that dripped off the food. "They don't call them 'breakfast cakes', do they? They call 'em *pan*cakes and pan is just the Greek word for 'all', which means you can eat 'em *all* the time."

"Are you nuts?" Theodore howled. "They call them

pancakes cos you cook them in a pan. Duh."

"Well, don't you just know everything, Theodore Dagget!" Mama Rose shot Charlie a wink and he couldn't help but laugh.

It was good to be home. Or at least Charlie felt that way until he saw Geoff Lench – Brooke's too-handsome, too-strong, too-*everything* boyfriend. The tall, blond boy bounded over. "Well, look who's back. It's Charlie Benja-traitor."

"Benja-traitor?" Theodore replied with a snort. "Was that supposed to be a joke? Because usually jokes have some element of *humour* in them."

"Shut up, Theo-*dumb*."

Theodore shrieked with fake laughter. "Theo... *dumb*! Genius! In fact... it's so funny that... I'm dying... from... hilarity..."

Theodore laughed so violently that he fell off the bench and on to the floor, where he twitched a few times and then went still.

"Ha, ha," Geoff said as he sat down next to Brooke. "Your friends are morons, you know that?"

"They're funny," she replied, "and I like them."

"Well, you're the only one. You really need to stay away from these clowns, Brooke – particularly the *exile*." He shot a withering glance at Charlie. "I leave tomorrow morning to start my job at the Division – Facilitator, Rank 1, thank you very much, hold the applause. They'll be asking you to come and join me soon, Brooke, if you just don't blow it."

"I haven't decided what I want to do yet," Brooke said, looking away.

"There he is!" a cheerful voice boomed out and Charlie turned to see a flash of colour scrambling up one of the giant branches of the Academy, partially obscured by wide, green leaves. "Charlie Benjamin, monster hunter!"

"Professor Xix!"

The giant, friendly Netherstalker leaped from the branch and on to the deck of the pirate ship. "Indeed it is. I've been missing you, lad. Good to see you whole and well!"

"I was just thinking the same thing about you! Hey – this is the first time I've ever seen you up in the tree."

"Because it's the first time I've ever been able to come here! With the Guardian's aura no longer preventing Nethercreatures from getting near the Academy, there's nothing to stop me any more. I quite love it, actually – so peaceful, so much *fun*. It makes me realise what I've been missing all these years, down in those dank Banishing caves, tending to my beasties." He absently cleaned one of his five eyestalks with a black, bristly foreleg. "To tell you the truth, I don't think I ever want to leave."

"Then don't," Charlie replied with a smile. It was good to see the Academy's Beastmaster so happy.

"Would you like some dinner, Professor?" Violet offered, gesturing to the pancakes.

"Don't mind if I do."

Quick as a blink, Xix snagged a cockatoo in mid-flight with a sticky line of webbing then yanked the squawking creature into his mouth in a colourful explosion of feathers.

"Delicious," he said, chewing loudly.

Geoff turned to Brooke in disbelief. "And this is who you want to hang out with instead of me? A bunch of dorks and a bird-eating monster? Unbelievable."

Suddenly, a portal snapped open beside them and several adults stepped through, all dressed in the starched uniform of the Nightmare Division.

"Charles Benjamin," a deep voice said. It was a voice they all recognised.

"Dad…" Theodore said weakly.

CHAPTER FOUR
EXILES AT THE ACADEMY

Theodore's father, William, stepped through the portal and on to the deck of the pirate ship. The medals on his black uniform gleamed in the sun, identifying him as the General of the Nightmare Division.

"What are you doing here?" Theodore demanded. Charlie had never heard him take such a stern tone with his father. It made him sound... older somehow.

"Why I am here does not concern you."

"But it concerns *me*," Mama Rose said, stomping up to the much bigger man. "In the Headmaster's absence, I'm the head honcho and I don't like fools portalling in and out of my tree. Now state your business or be on your way."

"All right," William said, then turned to Charlie. "Mr Benjamin, your presence at the Nightmare Academy suggests you are under the impression that you can return to your studies. Clearly, you do not understand the terms of your exile."

"I guess not," Charlie replied, "probably because no one has ever bothered to talk to me about it."

"Then let me clarify. You are no longer allowed on any property owned or controlled by the Nightmare Division – which includes the Nightmare Academy. You are to have no contact with anyone associated with either of these places, including your former fellow students." He glanced warningly at Theodore. "Further, you are forbidden from interfering in our battle against the monsters of the Nether. You may fight them in self-defence, but that is *all*. If you have any questions, everything is spelled out here in great detail." William held up a document with the words 'ORDER OF EXILE' written in bold at the top and signed by Director Drake at the bottom. He handed it to Charlie. "Read it carefully and follow it to the letter."

"Or what?"

William blinked, still holding the orders. "Excuse me?"

"I said 'or what'? What if I don't follow it? What are you *threatening*?"

Even Charlie was surprised by the depth of his anger. How dare Director Drake tell him where he could go, who he could hang out with and what he could and couldn't do to protect innocent people in this terrible War of the Nether? Drake was just a bureaucrat, a pencil-pusher – he didn't even have the Gift himself, but he certainly had no problem bullying people that did!

"If you violate any of the Rules of Exile, you will be Reduced," William said simply.

Charlie shrugged. "So what? Do you know how many times Drake has called for me to be Reduced? He's like a playlist with only one song."

Charlie expected William to argue back, but was surprised when the Banisher gently pulled him to one side, away from the others. "That may be, Charlie – but he really means to do it this time." For just an instant, Charlie could see through the tall man's gruff façade to the human being underneath. It was a welcome sight. "Most people were on your side before – you were just a child and the Headmaster was highly regarded. But no more. They're frightened now. The stakes are too high and almost everyone in the Division agrees that you're just too great a threat. They all *want* to see you Reduced, Charlie, and Drake is looking for any excuse to do it. If you violate these rules—" he held up the Order of Exile "—the Director *will* call on me to carry out the punishment and I *will* do it, do you understand?"

The General thrust the Order at Charlie, then turned to address the others. "From this moment on, Charlie Benjamin is never again to set foot here at the Academy and is forbidden from having contact with any of its students."

"That's not going to work for me."

Charlie stared in surprise at Violet. She was glaring at William with a hand on her hip and an expression that said, quite clearly, 'You don't scare me'.

"Whether or not it *works* for you, young lady, is irrelevant. It is simply a fact."

"No one is going to tell me I can't be with Charlie – I don't care what kind of 'orders' you have."

William frowned. "Well, you're welcome to join him in exile… although I do not recommend it."

"Then consider me exiled."

"Violet!" Charlie cried. As gladdened as he was by his friend's support, he couldn't bear the thought of being responsible for her getting kicked out of the Academy. Her mother was dead and her father was nowhere to be found. Without the Academy, what did she have left? "Don't do this. Really. I'll be fine."

"No, you won't. You'll be all alone."

"That's OK. It won't be the first time."

Violet shook her head. "No, it's not OK. When you

want to open a portal, what's the fear you summon up?"

Charlie hesitated. "Being alone, I suppose." He hated saying it out loud. It made him feel too… vulnerable.

"I won't let that happen to you, Charlie. Not now, not ever." She turned back to William. "You can tell Director Drake that I stand with Charlie."

"Me too."

All eyes turned to Theodore. He held his father's gaze with steady conviction. "Charlie's my best friend. I won't leave him. That's TI – Totally Impossible. You should know that." Charlie was about to protest when Theodore threw up his hand. "And don't even bother telling me 'no'. You know you're not going to change my mind, so don't even try. This is a Double-D."

"A Done Deal?" Charlie asked.

Theodore nodded and a smile broke through his stormy expression. "That's just the way I roll."

Charlie knew Theodore well enough to know that once his mind was made up, he wasn't easily persuaded to change it.

"OK," Charlie said. "And thanks. Seriously."

"Don't do this, Theodore," William said with a sigh. "Consider your actions carefully. The choices we make can have great and terrible consequences."

Theodore's eyes blazed with anger. "You mean like the way you *chose* to kill the Guardian and then decided to blame it on Charlie!"

The other students gasped in astonishment. There it was, out on the table – the *real* reason for Charlie's exile. William shifted uncomfortably, and Charlie was surprised by how unsettled the General looked in the face of his son's rage.

"That's not what happened."

"I saw you, Dad. I saw you there in the lair of the Named, killing the Guardian."

"You saw me *holding* it."

"Which is what killed it!"

It had been several weeks since Theodore had stumbled across his father in the icy lair of the Named. Charlie hadn't been with them then – he'd been in a nearby cavern, fighting the monsters of the Nether – but he could easily imagine the sight that had so tortured his best friend.

William, tall and strong, holding the limp body of the Guardian – a frail creature of great power, yet so desperate for human touch. But just as the Guardian's aura was poisonous to the creatures of the Nether, the touch of a human was poisonous to the Guardian.

"The Guardian was already dead when I got there,

Theodore. I told you that."

"I know you did. And you also told me that Charlie killed it."

"The *Director* said that."

A small distinction, Charlie thought. *But a very important one.*

"So does that mean you deny it?" Theodore pressed. "Or do you agree with the Director? When Charlie took the Guardian away from the rest of us, did he touch it and kill it?"

William's answer seemed to bring him pain: "Yes."

He's lying, Charlie suddenly realised. *He's not just mistaken – he's actively lying. He knows he's wrong, he knows I'm innocent, but he's doing it anyway. Why?*

And then the answer struck him like a thunderbolt.

Because he knows who really killed the Guardian – and he's protecting him. Charlie knew there was only one person in the world, aside from Theodore, that William Dagget would gamble his reputation to protect...

Director Drake.

No one saw who really killed the Guardian, but that was only because no one saw Director Drake slip out of the icy lair of the Named and enter the safe haven where the Guardian was holed up. No one saw him embrace the frail creature and press the poison of his skin against it, knowing that it would mean the Guardian's death.

No one... but Theodore's father, William.

"I don't believe you," Theodore said, staring at his father as Charlie and the rest of them looked on silently. "Whether or not you killed it, you had *something* to do with it. It definitely wasn't Charlie. Definitely."

"Son, listen to me..." William replied, clasping Theodore's shoulder with a strong hand.

Theodore shook it off. "Don't call me that. *Never* call me that again. I'm not your son." He turned to Charlie. "Let's go. Let's leave here and never come back."

Brooke stood up. "Well, if you're going, I'm coming with you."

"Are you crazy?" Geoff cried out. "Don't be stupid, Brooke! You're a Leet Facilitator – you're going to graduate in a few weeks and join me at the Division! Do you seriously want to throw that all away to go prancing around in exile with this... Noob?"

He spat the word 'Noob' at Charlie like it had a bad taste.

"He's not a Noob," Theodore said, stepping threateningly close. "He's an Addy, just like the rest of us. The Headmaster promoted us."

"The Headmaster!" Geoff laughed mirthlessly. "Is that old relic even still alive? No one's seen her in a week! I heard she croaked."

Even though Theodore wasn't strong, he was fast, and his small, bunched-up fist connected with Geoff's jaw almost instantly. Taken by surprise, Geoff dropped to the ground and Theodore pounced on him like a terrier, throwing punch after punch in crazy, windmill fashion.

"You take that back!" Theodore shouted. "She is not dead!"

Suddenly, Theodore felt a strong hand on his back as Mama Rose snatched him by the shirt and yanked him off the older boy. "Calm down, ya runt! I agree he needs a good butt-kickin', but now is not the time!"

"I'm going to knock you into tomorrow, idiot!" Geoff said, leaping towards Theodore. But before Geoff could make contact, a strand of spider-silk snaked through the air and wrapped around his leg. Professor Xix quickly reeled him in, slamming Geoff to the ground and dragging him backwards across the floor.

"Save the fighting for later, child," the Professor said calmly. "We've more important things to discuss."

Mama Rose turned to William. "Yeah, important things like what a sad and stupid piece of work you and the Director are. If I didn't have to protect these boys and girls here at the Academy, I'd join Charlie and his friends in exile!"

"Duly noted," William said softly.

"And you can add me to that list," Professor Xix seconded. "I would join them as well, if I didn't have to stay and care for my beasts."

"Well, we all have our priorities," William replied. "For me, it's the safety of all the human beings on this planet. For you, it's… well, I guess it's your *beasts*."

Xix's eyes darkened with anger and he was about to respond when a fiery portal popped open next to William and an adult Facilitator ran through.

"General Dagget?"

"Yes?"

"We need you right away, sir. There's been a development." The Facilitator suddenly looked very serious. "The fog over Central Park has lifted, General… and there's something *there*."

CHAPTER FIVE
THE CENTRAL MYSTERY OF CENTRAL PARK

A purple portal snapped open on the roof of the Plaza Hotel in Manhattan. Charlie Benjamin stepped through, followed by Violet, Theodore and Brooke. The tall, pretty girl sighed dramatically. "Well, this is typical. We've only been exiles a couple of minutes and already we're in trouble."

"How do you work that out?" Violet replied, barely even glancing at her.

"You heard General Dagget. He said that exiles aren't allowed to interfere in Nightmare Division business. Well... here we are. Interfering."

"We are not interfering!" Theodore said. "We're just *looking*. Heck, everyone on the planet is looking." He gestured to the news helicopters buzzing noisily overhead.

"Well, they've definitely got something to look *at*," Charlie replied, staring off at something the others couldn't yet see. "You better come and check this out. You won't believe it."

Everyone joined him at the edge of the hotel roof and looked down. A gigantic nautilus shell, easily five storeys high, towered over Central Park – its gleaming, pearly exterior stretched nearly from one end to the other. Thousands of snail-like creatures swarmed across it, secreting a glistening ooze from their bellies. The slime quickly hardened in the afternoon sun, adding yet another layer to the massive spiral. It was as ominous as it was beautiful.

Violet shook her head in amazement. "What is it?"

"Their new lair," Charlie replied. "At least that's my guess. But I don't know what those things are." He pointed to the snail-like creatures that were now slithering off the side of the shell and heading into the large opening in the end that faced the hotel.

"Shellweavers," Brooke replied. The rest of the group stared at her blankly. "Don't worry, there's no reason you'd know about them. I never saw one until Professor Xix showed them to us in our 'Building The Nether: Deadly By Design' class."

Charlie nodded. "OK. So what do they do?"

"Basically, they build things. Their slime dries as hard as steel. Harder maybe. Apparently, they constructed a couple of the palaces in the Inner Circle." She shrugged. "They're not dangerous."

"Maybe not," Theodore said. "But there's definitely something down there that *is*. Check out the soldiers."

He pointed to the hundreds of soldiers that ringed the park. Some stood – rifles at the ready – while others kept watch inside their tanks and military vehicles. The entire area was on lockdown. There were no civilians anywhere.

"Wow, they really want to keep people out," Brooke said.

"Or keep something else *in*," Theodore added. "Something like *that*."

He pointed to the entrance to the colossal shell. Something walked through the pearly curves, something regal and fierce.

"The Fifth," Charlie whispered.

Even from this distance, her alien beauty drew all eyes like a magnet. She was tall – nearly two metres – and her great mane of silver hair flashed brilliantly in the afternoon sun, spilling over crimson skin like a rain of steel on an ocean of blood. Her legs were long and strong and she had four arms, each ending in purple talons – the exact colour of her cat-like eyes. The

Shellweavers that slithered past her cowered as they tried to escape into the lair to shield their moist bodies from the heat of her ferocious glow.

The soldiers circling the park were instantly aware of her presence and they quickly grew quiet. Even the distant roar of traffic and the drone of the helicopters circling overhead disappeared, as if some giant creature drew in its breath and inhaled all sound and noise and clamour.

All silent. All still.

The Fifth opened her mouth and began to speak.

"Good people of Earth, I bid you welcome." Without even seeming to strain, her silken voice boomed up the sides of the skyscrapers and down the cavernous arteries of the city. "I have known many names. Some call me the Fifth; to my monstrous babies I am known as Mother; others call me Pearl – in honour of my marvellous new home." She gestured to the spectacular shell behind her with a flick of her top right hand. "But I invite *you* to call me by my real name – the Queen of Nightmares."

She smiled slyly. Charlie knew from grim experience that there was death behind that smile – death and suffering.

"She's beautiful..." Theodore whispered. Violet

stared at him incredulously. "In a totally creepy and evil way, of course," he quickly corrected himself.

"I understand you've all had a… difficult… week," the Queen of Nightmares continued with mock sympathy. "I'm told my darling babies visited you in the dark of the night with their pointy teeth and sharp stingers and caused you no end of trouble – children screaming, grown-ups carried off into the blackness. Terrible times…"

She shook her head sadly, although Charlie detected more than a hint of amusement.

"I am here today to tell you that the misery you have experienced is only the beginning. You have barely begun to taste the doom that will descend upon you. Today, *this minute*, things are going to change. And when they do, when you realise the full scope of the horror that is coming to your world, you will scream for the gentle days when all you had to fear were the beasts of your nightmares."

She raised her four arms. "Good people of Earth, your rule is over. The time of the monsters has come."

Oh no, Charlie thought. *What's she going to do?*

But before anything further could happen, there was a sound. Small at first – a low, dull whine – it soon sharpened and became the bright roar of a fighter jet screaming overhead. As it passed, two long, silver tubes launched from its wings and arrowed down towards

Central Park far below, leaving twin trails of smoke.

Missiles! Charlie realised. *They're going to shoot her with—*

WHAM! The explosion was so immense that Charlie and his friends were thrown to the ground as a wave of heat blasted them. A ball of fire blossomed out from the front of the enormous nautilus shell and plumed upwards, revealing a scorched crater beneath. As Charlie scrambled to his feet, he saw that the shell itself was untouched – the massive explosion hadn't seemed to damage or harm it in any way.

"Well, I'm no chef," Theodore said, shakily standing, "but I'm guessing that four-armed chick's goose is *cooked*." He turned to help Violet and Brooke up, while Charlie peered into the thick black smoke that blanketed the front of the shell, desperately looking for any signs of movement.

Nothing. And then he heard a sound.

Laughter. A female voice – rich and throaty and full of mockery.

As the smoke cleared, he saw the Queen of Nightmares standing exactly where she had been when the missiles first slammed into her: untouched and unharmed. Her purple cat-eyes glittered with dark delight.

"Charming," she said, and her casual tone of voice chilled Charlie to the core. "What's next? Poison? Lightning bolts? Asteroids? Please, send me your worst… as long as I get to do the same." With that, she raised all four arms to the sky. Her silver hair flashed in the sun. "Wonderful people of Earth, it's time to introduce you to my newest babies… my dark darlings… my Elemental Golems. Say hello to… Fire!"

With a flick of her top right hand, two circles of glowing cinder on the scorched earth beside her erupted into brilliant flames. The fiery pillars raged upwards, growing and expanding, licking at the sky with orange tongues until forming themselves into creatures. They were blazing, brutish things, five storeys high and made entirely of fire. Every step of their thick legs left behind bubbling pools of lava and every touch of their fingers summoned an inferno.

Violet shook her head. "This is bad…"

Then, with a flick of her lower left hand, the Queen of Nightmares made the ground shudder violently. Two huge slabs of rock exploded from the still smoking dirt and then crashed back down with earthquake-like force. Deep cracks spider-webbed across them, causing huge boulders to fall as if chiselled away by some insane, invisible sculptor. Giant stone creatures emerged. They were horrible, blocky things with wide foreheads and fists the size of tanks. Their dull, empty eyes made them look stupid and slow, but Charlie guessed that they were deadly.

"Ladies and gentlemen," the Queen of Nightmares said pleasantly. "Meet Earth."

The two Elemental Earth Golems walked to stand beside the two Elemental Fire Golems. With every step they took, the world shook with thunder.

"Um, wow," Theodore said. Charlie and the others nodded in agreement.

The Queen of Nightmares continued. "As all good schoolchildren know, there are not just two elements – there are four. I'd now like to introduce you to Air."

With a flick of her bottom right hand, the air on either side of her began to spin violently.

"And Water."

With the slightest of gestures from her top left hand, the water in the Pulitzer Fountain at the southern end of Central Park shot upwards, twisting and churning, until it split to create two gigantic spouts, each thirty metres high. The enormous columns of water and air expanded and reshaped themselves until they formed entirely new Golems, huge and terrible. Their existence was impossible, and yet, there they *were*.

The two violently spinning Water Golems sailed back to the shell on a giant wave that would have doomed even the most experienced surfer, while the two Air Golems – looking for all the world like living tornadoes – settled down on either side of their fellows to create a line of eight Golems, two of each kind.

Brooke stared at them in dismay. "Even if we destroyed all the regular monsters of the Nether, the Fifth could just create more of these things!"

Charlie nodded. "Yeah. And we don't even know if she can be killed. I mean, not even a missile strike could take her out."

"Oh, you'll kill her," Theodore said, arms crossed. "Definitely."

"How?"

"Well, how am I supposed to know? I'm sure you'll figure *something* out. I mean, that's what you do, isn't it? You're good like that." He clapped Charlie on the back.

Before Charlie could reply, the Queen of Nightmares lowered her arms and said, "Delicious people of Earth, the time for talking is over. Now is the time for dying." She turned to the Elemental Golems. "Attack, my beautiful babies."

As if turned on by a switch, the eight horrific creatures headed out of Central Park and into the city beyond. The military personnel that ringed the park held their ground and fired upon the rampaging monsters, but their bullets passed right through the Air, Water and Fire Golems and bounced off the Earth Golems like grains of sand off steel.

One of the Earth Golems shattered the large glass cube above the Apple Store on Fifth Avenue with a gigantic stone fist, followed instantly by a Water Golem that flooded down into the exposed complex beneath. A Fire Golem breathed lava on the nearby FAO Schwartz Toy Store, while an Air Golem rocketed high into the air and crashed down into Times Square, sucking soldiers into its deadly, whirling funnel.

As the Golems wreaked their destruction, Nethercreatures swarmed up from the sewers and down from the skies to attack the fleeing, panicked people. Dangeroos stuffed some of them into their stinking pouches while Hags descended, cackling, from the smoke-darkened sky to carry off others in a swirl of filthy hair and tattered ballgowns.

"What do we do?" Brooke screamed as they watched the devastation from their vantage point atop the Plaza Hotel.

Charlie shook his head. "Nothing."

"Nothing!" Theodore shouted. "What kind of an answer is that? Come on – let's go spank these bad boys!

Use some of those sweet Double-Threat moves you've been working on!"

Charlie pointed towards a purple flash far below. It was a portal created by a Nethermancer, who leaped through, followed by a mace-wielding Banisher. "They don't need us. The Nightmare Division is already sending in the troops. In fact, there's your dad—"

Charlie nodded down the street to a black-clad Banisher swinging a two-handed sword at a Silvertongue.

"OK, great!" Theodore shouted. "My dad's here! The cavalry has arrived! Woo-hoo! Now let's go and help out!"

"We don't have time. There's something much more important that we have to do first. We've got to—"

"CHARLIE BENJAMIN."

Charlie looked down to see the Queen of Nightmares standing in front of the giant nautilus shell. She smiled as her voice boomed across the city. "People are dying around you by the hundreds. Will you save them? Or are you *afraid*?"

"I'm not afraid," Charlie replied. "But getting rid of your 'babies'," he gestured to a Fire Golem that was climbing the Empire State Building, turning everything it touched into molten slag, "isn't going to solve anything. I don't need to stop them, I need to stop *you* – or you'll just keep making more of them."

"Very true. There's a whole world out there to destroy – a monster's playground – and my beautiful babies will soon rule it all."

"Every playground has bullies and every bully has a weakness. We'll soon find yours."

The Queen of Nightmares' laughter pealed across the skyscrapers, shattering glass. "Of course you will, Charlie Benjamin. Of course you will."

With that, she walked inside her pearly lair and was gone.

"OK," Brooke said. "Nice creepy confrontation with the most deadly boss of the Nether. Now how were you planning on killing her exactly?"

"No idea," Charlie replied. Unfortunately, that was *true*.

"There you are!" a familiar voice suddenly roared from somewhere high above. Charlie looked up to see a portal hovering in the air over the nautilus shell in the park. It was so far away that he struggled to recognise the person looking through it – until he noticed the weathered cowboy hat the man wore.

"Rex!"

The cowboy smiled. "We been lookin' all over for you, kid. Shoulda' known we'd find you exactly where you're not supposed to be – messin' around with Miss Mega-Monster."

"I've got a lot of questions for you!"

"And I probably got answers for some of them, which is why you need to come see us! Portal over and do it quick – me and Tabby gotta get back to the Headmaster pronto."

He turned to go, heading into the bluish landscape of the Nether.

"Wait!" Charlie yelled. "Where are you guys?"

"Well, I don't exactly wanna shout out our super-secret location in front of the lair of the Fifth – but here's a little hint…" Rex leaned back and threw something towards Charlie. The small object sailed through the air, glittering as it spun. "See ya soon, kid!" the cowboy shouted as the portal began to snap closed. "And *hurry*!"

Charlie leaped forward to catch the baseball-sized 'hint' that Rex had thrown.

"Well?" Theodore asked, leaning in. "What is it?"

Charlie showed them. It was a snow globe, and the plastic snow inside seemed to be swirling around a familiar-looking building.

"Isn't that Buckingham Palace?" Violet asked.

Charlie nodded. "Looks like it. Hey, Theo – think you can whip us up a portal to take us there?"

"Can I whip you up a portal?" Theodore echoed with a snort. "Hello? This is Theodore 'Portal' Dagget you're talking to – I whip up portals like pastry chefs whip up soufflés! One delicious, nutritious portal coming right up!" He closed his eyes and began to focus on his core fear.

As he did, Charlie looked out across the city to see many *other* portals popping into existence like embers from a windswept campfire – the Nightmare Division was clearly sending in the troops. Suddenly, a blue axe flashed in front of him, followed by two large, mosquito-like creatures that thudded to the roof, dead. Charlie recognised the beasts almost immediately – Bloodsuckers. They speared you with their long, sharp noses and sucked you dry, like a juice box.

"Thanks!" Charlie said, turning to Violet, who was wielding her axe. "I was sort of drifting and I didn't even see—"

But Violet wasn't listening to him. A cloud of Bloodsuckers boiled down towards them from the smoky sky and, as each one arrived, she chopped it up without thought or pity. Charlie loved to watch Violet Banish – a calmness descended over her as she moved with an almost machine-like precision: elegant, exact and lethal.

"How's that portal coming?" Brooke asked, turning to

Theodore. "No hurry, as long as you don't mind getting carried off by giant mosquitoes or spending some close, personal alone time with Mr Tornado."

She pointed to an Air Golem as it spun towards them from the destruction it had wreaked in Times Square. Its eyes were like twin hurricanes.

"Ye of little faith," Theodore replied.

Just before the Golem slammed into the Plaza Hotel in a massive explosion of concrete and steel, he snapped open a portal. As the landmark structure collapsed around them, everyone leaped through the gateway, which hung in space like a balloon.

Moments later, the Plaza Hotel, which had stood for over a hundred years, was gone... and so were Charlie and his friends.

CHAPTER SIX
THE HIDDEN HEADMASTER

A fiery portal snapped open on the red brick in front of Buckingham Palace. Charlie stepped through first, followed by Violet.

"So where do you figure they are exactly?" she asked, glancing around.

"Don't know," Theodore replied, stepping through next, followed by Brooke. "But I bet the guys in the hairy hats do." He pointed to the main entrance of the palace. It was guarded by several bayonet-wielding men wearing red jackets and furry black hats. "Let's just tell them to bring us to the Headmaster before giant monsters destroy the world."

Brooke grinned. "We could do that... or we could try it *my* way."

"And which way is that?" Violet asked.

"The pretty girl way."

She walked over towards the nearest royal guard with her thousand-watt smile turned on full blast. "Hey there, soldier! I love your uniform... it makes you look so strong and tall." She leaned towards him. "So listen, we think a good friend of ours is a guest inside the palace. Can you help us find her?"

The guard stared straight ahead, unblinking, not responding in any way.

Brooke glanced at Charlie, baffled – being ignored was clearly something she didn't have much experience with. She turned back to the guard with a flip of her pretty blonde hair. "Hey, don't worry. *I get it*. You're just supposed to stand there like a statue. That's your job, right? Totally cool. You're rocking that look really well, by the way. So here's what we're going to do. I'll tell you who I'm looking for and you just whisper where she is – it'll be our little secret. Her name is *Headmaster Brazenhope*."

No reply from the guard.

Charlie could tell from Brooke's expression that she was getting frustrated and he knew that when she got frustrated, she got angry and when she got angry—

"Look here!" the tall girl snapped. "I don't like this attitude! Now you better help us out this instant because if we don't get in there and see the Headmaster right away, giant monsters are going to destroy the world – comprende?"

"Hey, that was *my* plan…" Theodore mumbled.

"Comprende?" Charlie asked, walking up to her. "He doesn't speak Spanish, Brooke – he's British."

"Actually, I do know a little Spanish," the guard said defensively. He held his thumb and forefinger a few centimetres apart. *"Un poquito."*

"You talked!" Brooke shouted. "I knew you could!"

"Hey, kid!"

Charlie was startled by a man's voice high above. He looked up to discover Rex Henderson hanging out of a third-storey window, waving cheerily. Against the majesty of Buckingham Palace, the cowboy's glowing lasso and weathered Stetson made him seem like a page out of 'What's Wrong With This Picture'.

"Stop goofing around and get on up here! We got a lot to talk about!"

Charlie and his friends rushed inside, past the palace guard. As soon as they were out of earshot, the man sighed heavily. "Americans…"

Charlie had never seen anything as ornate as the inside of the palace. Elegant statuary and priceless paintings seemed to fill every nook and cranny.

"Hey, is that a Rembrandt?" Theodore said, pointing to a haunting portrait of a dour-looking man. He ran his fingers across it. "Look, you can feel the paint – it's real!"

"Of course it's real," a clipped British voice scolded. "And now it's 'real' *dirty*."

They all turned to see a thin, older man walking towards them with a puffy cloud of white hair atop his skeletal head. He was dressed in an extravagant purple suit – velvet by the look of it.

"Sorry about that, sir," Violet said. "That's just Theodore."

"And I am one of Her Majesty's valets. My name is Oscar."

"Like the Grouch?" Theodore blurted.

The man turned to him. "What an atrocious little boy you are."

"Exactly," Theodore replied, nodding. "Definitely atrocious."

"Believe it or not," Charlie said, "he's actually got a few good qualities."

"Perhaps we should mount an expedition to find them someday. Until then – follow me, please."

With that, Oscar strode through the maze of hallways

and stairs as the rest of the group struggled to keep up. Before long, they arrived at a heavy, hand-carved door. Oscar opened it and led the group into an elegant parlour filled with antique furniture. Rex was perched casually on the arm of a peacock-blue sofa that Charlie guessed cost more than his father had made in his entire lifetime. Tabitha Greenstreet stood on the other side of the room, her red, bejewelled hair perfectly framed by the pattern on the ivory wallpaper.

"There you are," Tabitha said, rushing to them. She hugged Charlie tightly. "We've been so worried."

"We're fine," Charlie replied. "But the rest of the world isn't doing too good. Have you seen what's going on with the Elemental Golems?"

Rex nodded. "Yup. Just when you think you know every Nethercritter out there, them fiends whip up some new ones to throw at ya. It's… it's *wearying*, is what it is."

"May I get you anything?" Oscar asked. Then, with the slightest of devilish grins, "A selection of cheeses, perhaps?"

"No more cheese!" Rex roared. "I mean, ya'll been unbelievably kind to us, but I'm about cheesed out. Everything here is cheese! Cheese selections, cheese sandwiches, cheese on toast. I had a dream last night where I was crushed under a giant wedge of cheddar cheese before being rescued by pirates from a cheese boat that was sailing on an ocean of melted cheese. In other words – no more cheese, ya got that!"

"Am I to understand," Oscar said mildly, "that you would not care for any more cheese?"

"Let me put it this way – if I ever ask for cheese again, I want you to—"

"Is there any way we could see the Headmaster?" Charlie interrupted. "We really need to talk."

The Headmaster lay propped up in bed in the room just off the parlour. Her normally brown skin looked waxy and ashen. She listened carefully as Charlie finished his story.

"So basically, we're exiled and not allowed to do anything or we'll get Reduced, but we have to do *something* because the whole planet's in danger."

The Headmaster nodded and Charlie detected a wince of pain. The wounds she'd suffered in the icy lair of the Named were grave, and she was still only in the beginning stages of recovery. Watching her now, Charlie flashed back to the last time he had seen her healthy and active – mowing down literally hundreds of Nethercreatures as they swarmed across her like ants on a sugar lump.

"The fate of the planet is in your hands," she said, her voice not much more than a whisper. "As you witnessed, the Fifth cannot be destroyed by any mortal means. Even weapons with a touch of the Nether on them, like yours—" she gestured to Charlie's rapier with a trembling hand "—won't harm her. To destroy her, you need one of the Ancient Weapons, forged in the Nether eons ago. You need the Sword of Sacrifice."

"Fine. How do we get it?" Violet asked. Her eyes were as flinty as the axe at her side and Charlie was struck once again by how hard she seemed now. The Banisher that stood beside him was a far cry from the gentle, artistic girl he had met just over six months ago.

"*You* don't get the sword, Ms Sweet," the Headmaster said softly. "Only a Double-Threat can wield something so powerful. And since Pinch has betrayed us and I'm clearly in no condition to get out of this bed, let alone fight, the task falls to Mr Benjamin, I'm afraid. But he cannot do it alone."

Theodore stepped forward. "We'll protect him – no problemo there. Nobody hurts Charlie Benjamin when Theodore Dagget is around. Nobody."

The Headmaster shook her head. "It's not your *protection* he needs, Mr Dagget. It's something far more precious. The Smith will explain it to you."

Charlie shrugged. "Who?"

"The Smith," Rex said. "As in blacksmith. You can find him in the Netherforge, out there in the mountains of the 3rd Ring. That's where Banishers go to make their weapons, and he's the fella in charge."

"Is that where you got your short sword?" Violet asked, gesturing to the one that hung from the cowboy's belt.

Rex nodded. "Yeah. The Smith showed me how to forge it, like he does for everyone – like he'll do for *you* someday, if there is a 'someday'." He turned to the Headmaster. "I can warn them not to touch him, right?"

The Headmaster smiled dourly. "It seems you just have."

"We shouldn't touch the Smith?" Charlie asked. "What will happen if we do?"

Rex sighed. "It would be... bad."

"Define bad," Brooke said. "Bad as in...?"

"Bad as in just don't do it or you'll hate yourself for the rest of your natural life!"

"Oh," Brooke replied, startled. "That kind of bad."

"Will you take us to him?" Charlie asked. "To the Smith, I mean."

Rex nodded. "Course I will."

The Headmaster shook her head solemnly. "That's not possible, Mr Henderson – you *know* that. They must go without you. The seeker of the blade must bring with him his three closest friends."

"Rex and I are his friends," Tabitha replied. "We're as close to him as anyone."

"No. You are his *mentors* – and there are only two of you. I know you don't wish to see the children suffer… but if they do not, the *world* will suffer."

Brooke looked a little queasy. "Excuse me, Headmaster, but exactly in what way will 'the children' suffer?"

"Soon you will understand, Ms Brighton."

Suddenly, the parlour door opened and Oscar rushed in. "I'm terribly sorry for intruding in this manner, but there's been a rather dramatic development. Something quite horrific is happening."

He picked up a remote control and turned on the wall-mounted television. As a newscaster babbled hysterically, live pictures from four major cities around the world flashed up on the screen.

In Spain, Air Golems stormed across a large bullring (helpfully identified as the Plaza de la Maestranza). The red dirt in the centre of the arena was funnelled up into the giant, rampaging creatures, turning them a dark, dusky colour. Screaming patrons tried to flee, but soon found themselves hurled miles across the heart of Seville by the tornado-like force of the monsters. Charlie was astonished to see a bull flung into the wall of the stadium, where it hung by its horns like a dart in a dartboard.

On another corner of the screen, Charlie saw Fire Golems smashing through the heavily fortified walls of Red Square in Moscow. The terrible creatures headed for the colourful spires of the Kremlin where they vomited up great geysers of lava. As they went about their destruction, they all but ignored a Russian military brigade that desperately tried to gun them down.

In Japan, Earth Golems raged through the neon jungle of Tokyo, yanking whole buildings from their foundations and raining debris on the screaming people below. The catastrophic scene looked horribly familiar until Charlie realised that it reminded him of the old Godzilla movies he had seen with his father – the giant lizard tearing apart the city in much that same way that these real-life beasts were doing now.

Finally, the last image on the TV showed Water Golems erupting from the River Thames and spilling across London. The terrible creatures washed away hordes of tourists as they snapped pictures of Big Ben and quickly drowned the onlookers who ringed Buckingham Palace.

Buckingham Palace.

"They're here," Oscar said, staring through the

window. "We must leave. Immediately."

Charlie sighed. "I didn't think it would happen this fast. The Fifth is summoning Golems everywhere…"

"Which is why you and your friends must go," the Headmaster said. "You're the only ones who can stop this."

"I understand. We'll go, but if we leave you in the condition you're in right now, how will you ever protect yourself if—"

"The Headmaster will be fine," Rex interrupted. "Me and Tabitha will see to her safety, just like we been doing. You four best get going. And kid…" Rex looked like he wanted to say something serious to Charlie, to *all* of them, but instead he just sighed. "Well, it's been an honour."

Charlie hugged him as Tabitha opened a portal. Through it, they could see smoke and an eerie blue glow – it was a forge of some kind.

The Netherforge.

Tabitha gestured them through. "Go on… all of you… and be safe."

Without a word, Charlie, Theodore, Violet and Brooke stepped through the portal and into the Nether, to whatever dark destiny awaited them there.

Deep in the nautilus shell that stretched from one end of Central Park to the other, the Queen of Nightmares lowered her outstretched arms.

"And so it begins," she said wearily. She seemed tired, as if the summoning of the Golems had taken a hefty toll on her. With an exhausted sigh, she strode across the shimmering floor and took a seat on the magnificent pearlescent throne tucked away in the heart of her lair. Nethercreatures scuttled around her, Class 5s mostly, their monstrous bodies hideously out of place against the clean, swirling spirals of the palace the Fifth now called home.

But, as out of place as the monsters seemed, there was something – or some*one* – equally out of place among the monsters.

A boy.

A *human* boy.

Edward Pinch walked through the hive of beasts completely unafraid. His lack of fear seemed justified because none of the creatures appeared to even notice him – and the few that did gave him a wide, respectful berth. Although he looked young, Pinch was actually much older. His boyish appearance was the result of drinking Hydra's milk. The miraculous substance had returned him to when he was most powerful, back to the age of thirteen, back to before he was stripped of his powers by the terrible process of Reduction.

"It's done," he said. "The Inner Circle is emptied of Nethercreatures, my lady. They're all here on Earth."

The Queen of Nightmares nodded approvingly. "Good boy. As soon as my lovely Golems destroy the cities, the rest of my fierce babies will pursue every last human to their dying breath. You've done well, Edward."

Pinch nodded, but didn't move. The Queen of Nightmares eyed him curiously.

"What is wrong? Are you afraid that I might… dispose of you… now that you've completed my bidding?"

"Yes."

"Come." She opened her arms wide and Pinch walked to her, resting his head against the reptilian skin of her waist. She held him tightly. "You are the favourite of all my babies, Edward. I will never let anything happen to you. Do you understand?"

"I do. Thank you." Pinch's voice was soft and trembling.

Realisation suddenly dawned in the eyes of the ancient and terrible beast. "There is something else, isn't there? It's not enough that you be protected, kept from harm. You want something more. You want to be *powerful*, don't you?"

Pinch's eyes lit up like stars. "Yes... powerful... exactly!"

"You can open portals. None of the creatures of the Nether, myself included, can do that. Surely, that makes you special."

Pinch nodded. "Yes, but... I'm still..." He looked away, unable to say it.

"Human?"

The way she uttered the word made it seem as though she understood every fear and dream in Pinch's dark heart.

"Yes. Human and... small and... weak."

The Queen of Nightmares laughed then. It echoed hollowly around the glossy walls of the shell. "There is no need for you to be small and weak, my darling. That is the role humans have always given you. That is not the destiny *I* see for you. I see something far greater."

Pinch looked up at her hopefully. "Is there something that can be done?"

"Of course. If you trust me, I can make you... glorious."

With a sharp talon, she slashed open the index finger of her lower left hand. Green blood oozed to the surface in a noxious bubble. She held the bloody finger to Pinch's small, thin lips.

"Drink," she commanded.

Pinch looked up at her, unsure. "Is it—"

"Drink," she repeated, more gently this time. "Drink and you will know power such as you have *never* known." The green bubble trembled on the tip of her finger.

"Yes," Pinch said, more confidently now. "I will." He leaned down, wrapped his lips around her bony finger and drank.

PART TWO
SWORD OF SACRIFICE

CHAPTER SEVEN
THE
NETHERFORGE

The craggy mountains of the 3rd Ring seemed to shift and shimmer in the blue light of the Netherforge. Charlie and his friends shielded their eyes from the glare as they stepped through the portal and on to the rocky ground. The hiss of steam escaping from underground vents and the ringing of hammers on metal filled their ears.

"Wow, just *look* at this place," Brooke said. "I had no idea it was this big."

The size of a football field, the Netherforge was built around a large well filled with a thick blue liquid that glowed like lava. The well was ringed by various ancient tools and machinery.

At one end was a crusher of some sort, dusted with a fine yellow powder from the shards of mustard-coloured crystals that lay shattered around it. Charlie recognised them almost instantly – he had seen those crystals on the 5th Ring. Large vats of water surrounded the forge itself. Charlie didn't notice any nearby springs to feed them, so he guessed that the water had to be brought in from the ocean of the 4th Ring – no easy task. A series of dark metal racks held stone moulds in the shape of weapons – swords, axe blades, lances – and everywhere Charlie looked, he could see oversized anvils.

"Man, this place is seriously awesome!" Theodore exclaimed. "Lots of danger!"

As their eyes adjusted to the intense blue light, Charlie and his friends noticed several Banishers busily working around the forge, crafting or repairing weapons. Charlie recognised German writing on the uniform of a man pouring some kind of molten metal into a mace-shaped mould. A woman with a patch that appeared to have Swedish writing on it pulled a glowing blue longsword from the lava and thrust it into a vat of water, where it sizzled in a geyser of steam.

"NO, FOOL!" a voice suddenly croaked – it was deep and thick with phlegm.

Charlie turned to see a large creature leaping across the forge. It landed on the stone with webbed feet, then rose to its full height – easily twice Charlie's size.

"What is that thing?" Brooke asked.

"I'm guessing it's the Smith."

The Smith was a giant bullfrog. Its grey-green skin was horribly pocked and scarred. A cartoonishly wide head rested on a neck that ballooned outward as it breathed. The beast's lips were green and rubbery and its eyes were cruel red globes that protruded from a face oozing pus. The creature snatched the longsword from the bewildered Banisher and proceeded to yell at her in Swedish.

"He doesn't look very friendly," Violet said.

Theodore snorted dismissively. "Aw, he doesn't scare me. And he better not yell at *us* that way. If he tries to, I will pulverise that overgrown frog! I'll Nether-Slap him!"

"WHAAAAT?" The swollen head of the great creature swivelled towards the boastful boy. "What did you – *crooooak!* – say to ME?" With one mighty leap, the Smith cleared the forge and landed centimetres from Theodore, who stumbled backwards.

"I, uh, I didn't mean anything by it, sir. Or at least, I didn't think you'd hear me."

"I hear EVERYTHING, boy! This is MY forge. I am the – *crooooak!* – SMITH!"

"It's a pleasure to meet you, Mr Smith," Brooke said, her voice quaking.

The Smith looked at her disdainfully. "What are you

CHILDREN doing here? This is a serious place for – *crooooak!* – SERIOUS Banishers." Then he noticed Violet's axe, which glowed a dim blue. "How DARE you bring such an inferior trinket to my forge. Is it a TOY? No toys here – WEAPONS! Serious weapons!"

"That's what we've come for," Charlie said. "A serious weapon. Maybe the most serious."

The Smith swivelled its balloon-like head in Charlie's direction. Its red eyes narrowed to slits. "You're different. There's something ABOUT you, boy. Something…"

"My name is Charlie Benjamin."

The Smith's eyes widened. "Ah, I've – *crooooak!* – HEARD of you." Charlie's ego flared pleasantly, but was quickly doused when the Smith continued: "I've heard you've caused great TROUBLE. I've heard you've caused much – *crooooak!* – TRAGEDY!"

"That's not true!" Theodore shouted. "It's all lies from people who don't know him, people who envy him!"

"And what say YOU, Benjamin? Is it all – *crooooak!* – LIES?"

"It's true I've made some mistakes," Charlie said, "and I'm sorry for those. But I never meant to harm anyone. We came here to save people – all of us."

"How NOBLE!" the Smith sneered. "Please, I BEG you, how can a simple smith like me be of assistance to such a – *crooooak!* – WORTHY group as yourselves?"

Charlie took a breath to steady his nerves. "We need a sword. The Sword of Sacrifice."

The Smith stared at him for a moment, then burst into cruel laughter. "Begone, CHILDREN, and waste my time no – *crooooak!* – further." It turned to go.

"Stop," Charlie commanded. "I need that sword – and you're going to get it for me."

The Smith turned back to him with a look of astonishment in its bulging eyes. "Oh, AM I?"

Charlie nodded. "Headmaster Brazenhope sent me here. She said I needed the sword to slay the Fifth. She said you would give it to me."

The Smith grunted. "Do you know, boy, what that sword would DO to you if you were to TOUCH it?" The creature leaned in so close that Charlie could smell the sour pus that dripped down its cheeks. "It would DESTROY you. Only a DOUBLE-THREAT can wield such a – *crooooak!* – magnificent weapon."

"I am a Double-Threat."

"Oh, really?" The Smith seemed far from convinced. "I'd HEARD that you were, but seeing you now, I find it HARD to believe."

"He is!" Theodore shouted. "He'll prove it to you!"

"Oh, he WILL," the Smith spat. "He will prove it – *crooooak!* – or DIE."

"Why does everything in the Nether have to end with 'or die'?" Theodore grumbled as the group followed the Smith up a treacherous trail carved into the face of the tallest peak on the 3rd Ring.

"I hate this," Brooke said, clinging to the mountain face for protection as she slowly edged her way upwards. She glanced down at the distant rocks below and turned ghastly pale. "Oh, boy, do I hate this!"

"Move it, Brooke," Violet said – the height didn't seem to bother her in the least. With the sure-footedness of a mountain goat, she quickly slipped past the tall girl and sprinted up the path to join the boys.

"In HERE!" the Smith shouted. The bloated creature stood at the mouth of a tunnel where the trail came to a dead end. "Not far NOW! The time of BANISHING is near!" With a boisterous *crooooak!* it hopped into the entrance – little more than a crack in the side of the mountain – and was soon gone.

Theodore stared into the blackness nervously. "Umm… looks kind of dark."

Charlie clapped his friend on the shoulder. "Don't worry. It'll be cool. Nothing to be afraid of."

"Afraid?" Theodore laughed shrilly. "Who said anything about afraid? Where did the word 'afraid' come into the conversation? I'm not afraid! I am a death-dealing machine! I am a weapon of doom!"

"You want me to go first?"

"Would you?"

Charlie entered, followed by Violet.

By then, Brooke had caught up. She peered uncertainly inside the mouth of the cave. "We're really going in there?"

Theodore swallowed hard and nodded. "Looks like it."

Brooke took his hand. "You'll protect me, right?"

Theodore instantly brightened. "Protect you? Are you kidding? This is Theodore Dagget you're talking to – the man with the plan! I eat Nethercreatures for breakfast! I—"

As he talked, he led her inside, praying desperately that she couldn't see his knees shaking. The tunnel, though dark, was mercifully short and Theodore was still babbling away when he and Brooke walked out the other side and into the pale blue light of the Nether.

"—and that's, of course, the benefit of my constant

chatter. See, it lets any Nethercreatures in the tunnel know that there's an instrument of destruction nearby and that they do not, repeat, do NOT want to tangle with him."

Brooke nodded sympathetically. "You were very brave."

"I know."

She tried to let go of his hand, but Theodore clung on tightly.

"Over here!" Violet shouted, breaking the awkward moment.

Brooke and Theodore scampered across the wide ledge they now stood on to join the rest of the group, who were waiting for them in front of a stone bridge that arched across a chasm. Clearly a natural formation, it had no guard rails, no steps, no protection of any kind.

The Smith turned to them with a dark expression that Charlie figured was its version of a smile. "So, my little GRUNTS, have you ever faced a – *crooooak!* – Chasm Wyrm before?"

Charlie shook his head. "Never even heard of one."

"I have," Brooke said. "They mentioned them in Leet Bestiary class. They're pretty rare, I think. They fly and… there's something unusual about them, but I can't quite…" She struggled to recall exactly *what* was unusual about them, then finally gave up and shook her head. "I don't remember. It's definitely *something* though."

Violet nodded. "Well, that's helpful. At least now we know it's 'definitely something'." She turned to the Smith. "So do you have any info about fighting these monsters, other than that there's 'definitely something' about them?"

"Only THIS: most Banishers – *crooooak!* – do not SURVIVE the encounter. Even DOUBLE-THREATS are undone by them." It hopped closer to Charlie, grinning. "I have been here eons, BOY. I have seen MANY – *crooooak!* – Double-Threats. I have seen many DIE!" The creature gestured to the bone-white rock that spanned the chasm. "Go on. Show us your – *crooooak!* – POWER."

Charlie glanced at his friends – then headed out over the arch.

"Good luck, Charlie," Violet called after him.

"And don't look down!" Brooke added.

"You just call me if you need help!" Theodore yelled. "I'll come running! You know I will!"

Charlie could hear them, but already his mind was drifting away, drifting to the solitary place he always went to when battle was imminent. Walking across the narrow bridge reminded him of something. At first, he couldn't quite put his finger on it, but then the answer came to him.

The Trout of Truth.

To be tested by the great fish, you had to walk alone across a series of stepping stones, until you reached the very middle of the fathomless black lake that the creature called home. There, you stated your destiny. If you spoke true, you were left unharmed. But if you lied, the Trout of Truth exploded up from the water and swallowed you whole before spitting you back out, covered in slime, on the far, grassy shore.

Glancing around, Charlie thought it was entirely possible that something might shoot up from the dark, airy depths beneath him and swallow him whole, just like the Trout of Truth – but he seriously doubted that it would have the generosity to spit him back out, unharmed. He stopped in the centre of the bridge and waited, his right hand resting on the hilt of his rapier.

It began to glow blue. Something was coming.

Charlie looked down into the chasm, straining to see movement in the darkness, trying his best not to be frightened by the nauseating thinness of the ribbon of rock on which he stood. Accidentally, his right foot knocked off a pebble. It fell into the inky well and Charlie waited for the sound of it hitting the bottom to echo back up at him. The sound never came.

But something else did.

Floating up from the darkness, Charlie saw one of the most beautiful sights he had ever witnessed. It looked like a giant butterfly, with a wingspan as wide as a cathedral ceiling. And the colours! Candyfloss pinks side by side with the brilliant green of a peacock's feather; swirls of sunset red next to the haunting purple of a twilight sky. The wings were a rainbow of hues, shimmering and shining against the blackness like a stained-glass window. As the creature rose, Charlie began to see the fine details of its pixie-ish body – wide, round eyes and an elfin nose. The creature smiled at him and the smile warmed him from the inside, filling him with its rosy glow.

This couldn't be the monster he was supposed to fight. Could it?

Greetings, traveller, the creature said, although its lips didn't move. Charlie wasn't sure if it actually spoke the words or if it somehow just transmitted them into his brain. *You look weary. You have been through many trials. You deserve rest… and comfort.*

The creature's voice was kind and soothing and Charlie was surprised to discover that he *was* a little bit weary and that he *did* need rest and comfort. Luckily, it looked like those were two things a marvellous being like this could provide.

"You're right," Charlie said finally. "I guess I am a little tired. Really tired, actually. People are expecting a lot of me – saving the world and all. Sometimes I just want to say 'forget it' and lie down and take a nice, long nap."

Back on the ledge, Theodore watched his friend with growing agitation. "What's he doing? Why is he having a heart-to-heart conversation with that monster? Why doesn't he just kill it?"

"I don't know," Violet replied, clearly concerned as well. "That thing is hideous."

Even though, to Charlie, it looked like a beautiful butterfly, his friends saw it for what it really was – a Chasm Wyrm. A flying red dragon with lidless green eyes and rows of razor-sharp teeth that stuck out of its black gums at crazy angles, like headstones in an ancient cemetery. Its tail was long and clubbed at the end and its wings were coated in hard scales that gleamed dully in the weak light of the Nether.

"Uh-oh," Brooke said.

Violet turned to her. "Uh-oh? Elaborate, please."

"I just remembered what the deal was about Chasm Wyrms. They take over your mind. They can make you think things that aren't real and do things you wouldn't ever want to do if they weren't in your head, controlling you."

"Information we could have used sooner!" Theodore

said. "Great. Now we've got a killer dragon getting ready to use Charlie like a meat puppet. Fun times!"

Back on the bridge, Charlie gazed at the giant butterfly in something like wonder. "Do you think it's safe for me to take a little nap right here?"

Charlie wasn't sure if he'd actually spoken the words or just thought them – but that didn't really matter, did it? The important thing was that the creature seemed to *understand*.

Go to sleep, it whispered in his head. *You will be safe. You will be protected*.

"Sounds good. I'm dead tired."

Charlie dropped to his knees, preparing to lie down. Out of the corner of his eye, he saw his friends leaping and shouting excitedly. He couldn't quite make out what they were saying, even though he was certainly close enough to hear them. Maybe sound travelled in a funny way over the chasm? That would explain it, although it didn't account for why he could hear the butterfly with no problem at all – the pleasant chiming of its voice seemed to fill his world.

What's wrong with them? Charlie wondered, staring at his friends.

They want you to jump, the butterfly-creature replied, *so that they can have me for themselves*.

"They want to steal you?" Charlie asked. And then he realised that of *course* they did! Who wouldn't want to possess something so beautiful? Greedy little thieves...

They'll never stop, you know. They call themselves your friends, but they really hate you. They want you dead.

"They want me dead," Charlie echoed. The shimmering creature's words were so clear and reasonable. He was astonished that he had never before realised how evil his so-called 'friends' really were. It was a shame that it had taken a marvellous being like the butterfly to open his eyes to the truth.

That's right – I do speak the truth. I would never lie to you. They're the ones who lie. They must be stopped.

"I have to stop them," Charlie said, rising to his feet. Yes, that felt right. Action was called for in such a dire situation, wasn't it? Extreme action.

You have to destroy them. It's the only way.

Charlie drew his rapier. "Destroying them is the only way."

He walked down the bridge to where his friends – who weren't really his friends, he was certain of that now – stood waiting. He knew what he had to do.

He had to kill them all.

CHAPTER EIGHT
THE
CHASM WRYM

Charlie walked towards Theodore with a mad gleam in his eyes, rapier at the ready. The monster flapped slowly behind him, like a kite on an invisible string.

"What's he doing?" Brooke asked, stepping back.

"I think the Chasm Wyrm got to him," Theodore replied grimly. "It looks like he wants to hurt us."

Violet turned to the Smith. "The Headmaster said we would suffer. Is this part of the test for the Sword of Sacrifice? Does Charlie have to sacrifice us in order to *get* the sword?"

The Smith grinned. "OH, I can't tell you that. It would spoil all the – *crooooak!* – FUN!"

Violet raised her axe to the creature's throat. "Answer me or I'll kill you right now. Look me in my eyes and see if I mean it."

"Oh, I can see you MEAN it, girlie. And you might be able to do it too – but not before HE – *crooooak!* – kills THEM!"

Violet turned to see Charlie swing his rapier at Theodore. Without thinking, she sprang between the boys and intercepted the blow with her weapon.

"Charlie! Stop it. You don't want to do this."

He answered with a flurry of strikes – quick, precise blows that Violet struggled to repel. In his extraordinarily talented hands, the weapon was a blue blur and it took every ounce of her skill to counter the blizzard of incoming attacks.

He's better than me, she suddenly realised. *I'm fast, but he's faster. I'm strong, but he's stronger. If this keeps up, we're all going to die by his hand.*

She stumbled backwards, barely managing to parry an overhead blow. "Theo! *Say* something to him! Wake him up!"

As Violet absorbed yet another round of slashes, Theodore stepped forward. "Charlie, we're not the enemy, we're your friends! I'm your best friend in fact. Your superhero sidekick, your closest compadre... Don't you remember?"

From somewhere far away, Charlie could hear the lanky boy yelling, but it was all just white noise – a TV tuned to a dead station. He waded in with fresh fury, landing blow after crushing blow, and he could tell that the girl – Violet, was that her name? – was beginning to lose hope. She knew she was outmatched and he could see the terrible realisation descending upon her like a storm cloud.

And why not? he thought coldly. *She can't possibly beat me. No one can. I'm a Double-Threat…*

"Listen to me, Charlie!" Theodore shouted. "That thing is messing with your mind! We've been friends for, like, for ever! Remember the first time we met on the pirate ship at the top of the Nightmare Academy, when the Headmaster kept dropping me into the Nether? Remember how *insane* that was?"

Theodore's voice buzzed in Charlie's ear like a mosquito. It was annoying in its insistence to be heard, but somehow, he *did* hear it. Way in the back of his mind, he vaguely recalled standing on the pirate ship many months ago as the Headmaster opened portal after portal under the squawking boy, sending him plummeting into the Nether. At the time it had seemed…

Funny?

Maybe. He wasn't sure. The only thing that was clear to him now was the threat he was currently facing from this girl – this Violet – who was almost, but not quite, as powerful a fighter as he was.

"You do remember!" Theodore yelled. "I can see it in your eyes." Charlie tried to push the yapping boy from his brain, but Theodore just wouldn't stop. "Do you remember what I said to you the first time I met you? I said we were going to be best friends. And do you know why? Because I knew it instantly. Never a doubt. And it was true! That's what we are. *Best friends.*"

Was it true? Charlie wasn't so sure.

The girl tried to force him backwards with a sword strike, but Charlie dodged it nimbly, then kicked her in the stomach, knocking the breath out of her. She dropped to her knees, the back of her neck exposed to his fiery blue blade. He raised it.

"The Trout of Truth!" Theodore screeched. "You remember how it kept swallowing me because I insisted I was a Banisher just like my dad? Man, that fish sucked!"

To Charlie's surprise, he *did* remember something about it. Seven times Theodore had claimed he was a Banisher – even though he was truly a Nethermancer – and seven times the giant trout had swallowed him whole and then spat him back up on shore, covered in goop. At the time, Charlie thought that anyone who was so determined to get their way was someone you definitely wanted on your side, someone who could potentially make a great friend.

He's not your friend, the magnificent butterfly spoke into Charlie's mind, its voice as soft and light as a cloud. *He's your enemy. He's the betrayer. He must die, just like the girl at your feet. All of them must die...*

Right, Charlie thought, thankful to be able to regain focus and return to the task at hand. His friends had to die. Well, not his 'friends' obviously – I mean, after all, you don't hurt your friends... Do you?

"Charlie?"

He turned to see a tall, blonde girl smiling at him. "Do I know you?"

"Yes," Brooke said, tentatively stepping forward. "You saved me in Barakkas and Verminion's lair, remember? It was a long time ago. We went there to rescue your parents."

Barakkas and Verminion's lair... saving his parents... that sounded familiar.

Charlie lowered his weapon. "That's right. But we did something else too, didn't we? What was it?"

Brooke smiled and blushed a little. "You mean this?" She leaned forward and gave him a kiss. It was startling... and quite nice. "We did that once before, on the beach. Do you remember?"

Charlie did. Her lips were soft and…

He nodded. "I do. You're… you're beautiful."

Don't be seduced, the floating butterfly said. *The girl uses her beauty to distract you. The boy pretends to be your best friend to confuse you. And the other girl uses her prowess as a Banisher to protect them from you. This is how they will defeat you: beauty, friendship, skill… Raise your weapon, boy. Strike! Kill them all!*

Violet held out her hand. "Help me up, Charlie."

He looked down at her and the dark cloud that had taken over his brain suddenly lifted, revealing the truth of who she was.

"I'm sorry, Violet," he said. "I… I don't know what came over me." He reached down and pulled her to her feet.

She smiled warmly. "It's OK. You did great. Amazing actually. You fought it off. I don't know if I could have."

STRIKE! the voice screamed in his mind. *KILL HER!*

This was no longer the soft, gentle sound of the beautiful creature that Charlie had seen rise up on shimmering wings. This voice was as jagged as shattered glass and as final as a hammer blow on a coffin nail. This was a voice of command – and it had every intention of being obeyed.

KILL HER! SHE'S WINNING!

Charlie turned round and, for the first time, saw the creature for what it truly was.

A Chasm Wyrm. Ancient. Evil. Deadly.

KILL HER! that horrible voice shrieked. *NOW!*

Charlie raised his rapier. "I think I'll kill you instead."

Even the Smith seemed shocked by what happened next. It looked as if Charlie... *twitched*. The movement was so subtle that it almost didn't look like he had moved at all, but that was only because Charlie had thrown his rapier faster than the human eye could see. The blazing, blue sword rocketed through the air like a javelin and drove right through the terrible Wyrm's left eye and into its brain. The creature shrieked and went limp, dropping to the stone bridge, which shattered under its weight. Charlie ran to the edge of the cliff and watched as the lifeless monster disappeared into the blackness of the chasm below. When it was gone, he breathed a sigh of relief and turned to the Smith.

"OK. I passed the test and lost my rapier in the process. Looks like I need a new sword. I'd be happy to take the Sword of Sacrifice as a replacement."

"I IMAGINE you would," the Smith croaked. "But we have barely even BEGUN the test. You have only proven yourself to be a BANISHER, boy. To be a Double-Threat, you must also prove that you are – *crooooak!* – a NETHERMANCER!"

Suddenly, the huge bullfrog opened its mouth and flicked out its long, pink tongue, slamming Charlie in the chest with the fleshy bulb at the end. He pinwheeled backwards towards the chasm, grabbing wildly for something to hang on to – but there was nothing to grab.

"Charlie!" Theodore screamed as he watched his best friend tumble, head over heels, into the yawning abyss.

Pinch's body burned with an inner fire.

More than an hour had passed before he began to feel the effects of sipping the blood of the Queen of Nightmares. He didn't know what to expect really – had no idea what drinking her blood would *do* to him. He knew only that he had spent his entire life feeling small and weak when what he really desired was power – raw and towering. The kind of dominance that the Named possessed before the Queen destroyed them.

But that wasn't the whole truth, was it? She had destroyed them, yes, but she had also *created* them to begin with.

Just as she was *re*creating Pinch.

It started as a tickle. He could feel it in his hands and

feet, a sort of prickly feeling. Soon it spread throughout his body before flaring into a dull ache. The ache turned warm, and then hot, and then became an excruciating roar, a blazing turbine, as if his entire body were being melted from the inside so that it could be reformed into something new.

There, in the very heart of the nautilus shell, the man named Pinch – who had recently regained his power by becoming a boy – was mutating. Once again, he was being transformed and, this time, he would not seek the approval of other humans.

This time, he would make them scream with fear.

"It's happening," the Queen of Nightmares said as Pinch's body began to bubble and stretch like molten plastic.

He looked down in strange fascination as hairy, red insect legs – six of them – poked through his skin. It didn't hurt really – the nerves in his flesh seemed to be dead now, which was lucky because everything from his chest down soon sloughed away like a snakeskin, revealing a bristly, segmented body beneath. Suddenly, that body began to grow with startling speed and Pinch was dizzied by the rapid change. Where, just moments ago, he had looked *up* at the Queen – now he looked *down* at her from an immense height. She smiled approvingly.

"Good, my beautiful baby. Look at yourself. See what you have *become*."

There was no mirror in the throne room, but the walls of the shell were a polished pearl and he could see his reflection in them. Pinch stepped back and gazed, for the first time, at his new form.

He had become an ant – but the world had never seen such an ant. This was no tiny creature that could be carelessly crushed under the heel of a boot. Pinch was a giant now, easily the size of a jumbo jet, and his hard carapace gleamed a toffee-apple red. Instead of an insectoid head, Pinch was pleased to see that his own face protruded from the massive body – his *adult* face. True, it was plated in a thick shell just like the rest of him, as red as a fire engine, but the torso and head were still undeniably... *Pinch*. His two arms, which ended in clawlike fists, were corded and powerful. He flexed them and was astonished by their strength.

"I'm... fearsome," he said, shocked at the gravel of his voice.

The Queen of Nightmares nodded. "Yes, you are, my baby. We all have a monster inside us. I just helped you to find yours."

"Will I stay this way?"

"For a time. Eventually, you will return to your weak

and pitiful former self. To regain your power, you will need to drink more. Upon your third taste of my blood, the change will become permanent and then no one will be able to harm you – not even that wretched boy, Charlie Benjamin."

Pinch smirked. "Unless he gets the Sword of Sacrifice, that is."

The Queen of Nightmares froze. Her eyes went cold. "What did you say?"

"The Sword of Sacrifice," Pinch replied, looking down at her. "It's one of the Ancient Weapons. It gets its power from the Nether Core and can slay any monster alive – or so it is said."

The Fifth pursed her lips. "Why did you not think to mention this delightful little tidbit before?"

Pinch laughed. "Because Benjamin will never get that sword, trust me. For him to attain it, his friends would have to pass the Test of Sacrifice. I have *seen* these friends. They will fail him."

"Perhaps." She walked away from him then and, when she next spoke, her voice was as cold and hard as a glacier. "Or perhaps they will surprise you, just as you are now surprised at having become the marvel I see before me. Life is… unpredictable."

Pinch sighed. "Indeed."

She walked back to him and lovingly stroked one of his massive legs. "You can't let him get that weapon, my dark darling. You must kill him before he does. *Promise me.*"

"It will be done," he replied. "I promise."

Moments later, the monster that Pinch had become opened a portal to the Nether – the only creature who could – then stepped through and was gone.

CHAPTER NINE
THE TEST OF SACRIFICE

Charlie fell into the abyss.

He had no idea how deep it was, but he knew that he had to find some way to safely bring himself to a stop or he would die. He thought about opening a portal to one of the oceans on Earth so that he could use the water to slow his fall, but quickly realised that that wouldn't work – at this speed, the water would be as hard as concrete and hitting it would kill him instantly. There had to be another way…

Strangely, his mind flashed to an image of Spider-Man slinging webs through canyons of skyscrapers, never having any problems with the treacherous falls he took.

Must be nice to shoot webs, Charlie thought as he plunged through the terrible dark. Then: *Shoot webs.*

Spider-Man. Spider shoots webs. And he knew what he had to do.

Charlie waved a hand and opened a portal directly beneath him. Through it, he had a bird's eye view of the Nightmare Academy. He plummeted into the portal and was soon hurtling through the air back on Earth, towards the great tree far below.

"XIX!" he screamed as the cold wind tried to steal the words from his mouth. "PROFESSOR XIX! ARE YOU THERE?"

Charlie saw several students from the Academy staring up at him in confusion – but Xix was nowhere in sight.

"XIX, IF YOU CAN HEAR ME, I NEED YOUR HELP! THIS IS CHARLIE BENJAMIN!"

The top leaves of the Nightmare Academy whipped past his face as he plunged through them, only seconds from slamming into the hard sand below.

"PLEASE, PROFESSOR! HELP ME!"

He was out of time. Either Xix was there and could save him or he was going to—

Something scuttled across a tree limb. Charlie saw a sticky strand of white webbing shoot out from between the leaves. It snaked around his feet and wrapped around a thick branch as he fell, pulling taut, stretching like a rubber band, slowing his descent.

"Thanks, Professor!" Charlie yelled, catching just the briefest glimpse of his old friend and teacher before hurtling past him towards the ground below.

"My pleasure, Charlie Benjamin!" Professor Xix shouted back.

Even though the silken strand was slowing his fall, Charlie realised it wouldn't be able to bring him to a stop before he slammed into the earth. Just as the hard sand rushed up to meet him, he opened another portal and dipped through it into the Nether, just a few metres above the wide ledge where the Smith stood. The webbing attached to his ankle stretched to its breaking point, slowing Charlie to an almost complete stop. With another wave of his hand, he closed the portal above him, snapping the silken strand in half, and dropped the remaining few metres to land harmlessly on the ground next to Theodore in a puff of dust.

Everyone stared at him, shocked.

"That was simply ridiculous," Theodore said finally. "Truly outrageous."

Charlie staggered to his feet, then turned to the Smith. "Well, does that prove to you I'm a Banisher *and* a Nethermancer?"

The bloated creature laughed its thick, phlegmy laugh.

"So you ARE a Double-Threat, BOY! Good. You have earned the right to TRY for the sword." It leaped towards the dark tunnel that snaked its way into the mountainside. "Follow me, ALL of you. It is time – *crooooak!* – for the Test of SACRIFICE!"

Charlie and his friends blindly groped their way through the blackness of the tunnel. The walls were moist and the air had a chalky smell.

"I can't see a thing…" Brooke complained.

"Yeah, well, just be careful you don't bump into the big, ugly frog," Theodore whispered. "It's probably not too far up ahead and, remember, Rex said touching it would be – and I quote – 'bad'."

"The big, ugly frog can HEAR you," the Smith croaked.

Charlie was startled to discover that the beast was only a couple of steps in front of him. "Are we close?" he asked.

"Almost THERE…" They heard a grinding of stone as an unseen door rumbled aside, allowing a shaft of blue light to spill into the tunnel. "Now… enter the CHAMBER of Ancient WEAPONS." They followed the creature inside.

The chamber glowed dimly blue, illuminated by the

same kind of lava that they had previously seen bubbling up from the well in the Netherforge. It ran through cracks in the floor. Charlie noticed that the Smith was careful to avoid touching the stuff.

"What is that?" he asked.

"The MAGMA? It rises from the – *crooooak!* – CORE of the Nether. It causes EXCRUCIATING pain to the monsters here. That's why they AVOID the Forge… and that's why we temper the BLADES in its terrible fire. The Ancient Weapons are filled with its POWER."

The Smith hopped from the small chamber into a large cavern. Charlie and his friends followed and were left literally breathless by the astonishing sight before them. Easily five storeys high, blue magma dripped down the sides of the rough stone walls, creating the impression of a star-streaked sky, an exploding constellation of glowing cobalt that rained down around them like fireworks.

And that wasn't even the most impressive thing. In the centre of the cavern stood a massive amber crystal, shining like a sun. And in the centre of the crystal was a sword of unequalled magnificence.

"The Sword of SACRIFICE," the Smith said darkly.

Charlie walked towards it, amazed by the craftsmanship. Seen through the crystal, the metal of the blade gleamed a brilliant turquoise and the hilt was fashioned from a wood so dark it looked almost black. There were carvings on it as well – pictures of monsters that Charlie had never seen before. A two-headed thing with hooks for hands. Something that looked like a snake walking upright.

What were these creatures? he wondered. Were they other Named? Beasts the blade had previously killed? Or something else entirely?

"It's incredible," Charlie whispered.

"AYE," the Smith croaked. "It IS. As the seeker of the blade, we begin with YOU. Come." The creature hopped to the far wall. Charlie followed and, as he neared it, he noticed a hole in the rock, about the size of a man's fist. "Put your hand INSIDE."

Charlie hesitated. The hole was dark and he couldn't see where it led. He put his ear to it. There was a buzzing sound.

"Uh, Charlie," Theodore said, walking up. "My dad wasn't around to tell me much when I was growing up, but one of the things he *did* tell me was 'never stick your hand in a dark hole, stupid'. Or something like that. Point is – if it were me, I wouldn't be putting my hand anywhere near that thing."

"Good ADVICE!" the Smith cackled. "Let's just end this charade and – *crooooak!* – go HOME."

Charlie glanced at Violet. Even though she was clearly concerned, she gave him a small, supportive nod.

Taking a steadying breath, Charlie stuck his hand in the hole, all the way up to the elbow. The buzzing sound intensified and, suddenly, he felt something on his hand. It was feather-light and had four feet that dug into his flesh like pinpricks – not painful but definitely unpleasant.

"There's something on me," he said, trying his best to stay calm. "I can feel it crawling around."

"Let's have a LOOK," the Smith replied. The others all leaned in as Charlie pulled his arm out.

"Ugh, gross!" Brooke exclaimed when she got her first look at the oversized purple wasp that clung to the back of Charlie's sweaty hand. Veiny wings spread out from a bloated abdomen that ended in a curved, needle-like point. It buzzed ominously. "Does that thing sting?"

"Oh, YES," the Smith said pleasantly. "Indeed, it DOES. It's called a SHOCK WASP."

The Shock Wasp crawled around Charlie's hand and on to his palm. A clear fluid oozed from the stinger on its back.

"Well, get it off him!" Theodore yelled. "It's going to hurt him! Here – I'll do it..." As he reached forward to swat the hideous thing, the creature suddenly reared back and plunged its stinger deep into Charlie's open palm.

"No!" Violet screamed.

The pain was immense – a red-hot spike of torment. Charlie could see the wasp's abdomen beating like a small heart as it pumped him full of poison. A horrible throbbing spread from the wound until it consumed his entire body, quickly followed by a welcome numbness. Charlie collapsed to the ground, unable to move.

"What's happening to him?" Violet demanded. "Is he dying?"

"He is PARALYSED," the Smith replied. Charlie's breathing came in harsh gasps as the wasp took wing and flew back into the darkness of its hole. "Do not WORRY. It wears off in time. He is quite – *crooooak!* – SAFE. Far safer than you are about to be, I'll WAGER."

"But why?" Theodore said. "Why did you do it to him?"

"So that he cannot – *crooooak!* – interfere with what is to come. His part in this little test is OVER. Yours is just BEGINNING." With one giant leap, the Smith hopped to the crystal that housed the sword. "The Sword of Sacrifice gets its name not from the SEEKER'S sacrifice – but from YOURS. If Charlie Benjamin is to – *crooooak!* – obtain it, you must prove he is worthy of the gift by giving up the thing that is most VALUABLE to you."

"How?" Theodore asked.

"I will TAKE it from you."

Brooke stormed up to the creature. "And what does that mean? The thing most valuable to us – how are we supposed to know what that is?"

"YOU don't," the Smith replied, a devilish gleam in its bulbous eyes. "But I DO. I will ask you if you wish to SACRIFICE. If you say yes, then you will LOSE something, something PRECIOUS, something… IRREPLACEABLE. So… who goes FIRST?"

Theodore and Violet glanced uneasily at each other. They both opened their mouths to speak, but Brooke beat them to it.

"Me."

Violet turned to her. "Are you sure? We don't know what's going to happen here. Maybe I should go first."

Brooke shook her head. "You two have helped Charlie in a million ways with your skills. Me? Going first is the… well, it's the least I can do." She turned to the Smith. "I'm ready."

Charlie was desperate to yell out: "Wait… let's consider this! We need to find out more! He's not to be trusted!" But his muscles wouldn't obey him and all that escaped his lips was a weak moan.

The Smith leaned in nauseatingly close to Brooke. "Do

YOU, Brooke Brighton, agree to SACRIFICE that which is most important to you so that Charlie Benjamin can – *crooooak!* – wield the SWORD?"

Brooke took a deep breath to steady her nerves. "I do."

Silence. No one moved. No one spoke.

What's happening? Charlie wondered.

A second later, he found out. With a gesture as quick as the strike of a snake, the Smith reached out and stroked Brooke's milky-white cheek with the tip of a pus-covered finger. She leaped back in disgust.

"Ugh, what did you do that for?"

She quickly wiped the slime off with the palm of one hand… but the damage had already been done. The skin the Smith touched began to change. It bubbled and darkened and then spread like wildfire across her exquisite face, leaving behind a pocked, greenish landscape of pitted flesh.

"Oh, no…" Violet gasped.

"What?" Brooke shrieked. "What's going on?"

"Your BEAUTY has always been the thing most important to you," the Smith said softly. "And now you have SACRIFICED it."

Brooke looked down to see that the horrible brackish colour was now spreading across her arms and hands. Her beautiful blonde hair fell from her head in thick clumps. "No! This can't be happening!" she moaned, turning to look at her reflection in the crystal beside her. A grotesque, reptilian face stared back – pocked, rubbery lips on a protruding mouth, bulging eyes, slits for ears.

Don't let the Smith touch you, Charlie thought with dismay and now he knew why. All along, Brooke had relied on her beauty… but that was gone. He wanted to hold her, comfort her, but he couldn't. Summoning all his strength, he managed to gasp out one word: "Sorry…"

"You're, you're SORRY?" Brooke shrieked, spinning round on him. "I look like a frog! I've been turned into a big, horrible, green *thing* just so you could get some stupid sword and now you're just – *crooooak!* – sorry!" She clamped a hand over her sticky lips. "Oh, my God, I just croaked! I croaked! I CROAKED!"

"Well, here's the good news," Theodore said. "True, you may have just croaked – which, I admit, is a little creepy. And you're definitely green and sort of reptile-ish, but you're not actually a *frog*. Not like he is, I mean." Theodore nodded to the Smith. "You look just like you did before, except now you're bald and have froggy-looking skin, but you're definitely *not* the kind of frog that lives in swamps and jumps over logs and eats flies. Definitely not *that* kind. You're the good kind." Theodore did his best to smile comfortingly.

"The *good* kind?" Brooke shrieked and, weeping, she ran to a corner of the room and curled into a ball.

"Good work, Theo," Violet said with a sigh.

"What? I was trying to be *nice*."

The Smith turned its large, bloated head towards him.

"It's now YOUR turn, boy. Do YOU, Theodore Dagget, agree to SACRIFICE that which is most important to you so that Charlie Benjamin can wield the SWORD?"

Theodore swallowed hard.

CHAPTER TEN
THEODORE TAKES HIS TURN

Theodore started to reply, but Violet clamped her hand over his mouth before he could.

"Don't say anything!" She walked up to the Smith, her face glowing amber in the light of the crystal. "Why are you making us suffer like this? Why are we playing games? Why don't I just kill you now and *take* the sword." She raised her axe threateningly.

"Whoa, whoa, whoa!" Brooke said, looking up, her pocked skin streaked with tears. "Wait a minute – *now* is when you decide to take a stand? Unbelievable! I mean, where was all this bravado two minutes ago when I still looked like a *human being*?"

"I'm sorry, Brooke. When he said he was going to take something valuable, I thought he meant an actual *thing* – an object. I didn't realise he meant… this." Violet gestured to Brooke's discoloured skin.

"Well, that's quite a – *crooooak!* – mistake! I'm so glad you saw the error of your ways before something bad happened to you and Theodore!"

"It's not like that..."

"Oh, really? You've always envied my beauty and now look at me! I'm hideous! This is probably the happiest moment of your life, isn't it? This is everything you've ever dreamed of!"

Violet shook her head. "No. I *hate* that this has happened. I just don't want to make it worse."

"Worse? Worse than *what*?" Brooke ran towards her. "This is no fairy tale! I'm not some transformed princess that's going to get kissed by a handsome prince and magically become beautiful again! Don't you – *crooooak!* – get it?"

"I do. And if there was anything I could do about it, I would. Tell me what you want me to do."

Brooke glared at her... but had no answer. "Just make him pay," she said before glaring at the Smith and skulking away.

"You're welcome to KILL me, young Banisher," the Smith croaked. "Or to TRY, but it won't help. The sword will only release from the crystal at MY command. Even if I am dead, the price SHE paid —" the creature glanced at Brooke "—will STAND, the weapon will be lost to you for ever and the world of HUMANS will most certainly FALL!" The Smith leaned in close, its diseased nose nearly touching Violet's. "Go ahead, girl... make a MOVE."

Violet glared at the beast and Charlie was pretty sure she was going to take a swing... but common sense seemed to get the better of her. Without another word, she turned and walked away.

The Smith chuckled and then focused its burning red eyes on Theodore. "Once again, BOY, I ask – do YOU, Theodore Dagget, agree to SACRIFICE that which is most important to you so that Charlie Benjamin can – *crooooak!* – wield the SWORD?"

What could the horrible creature want from Theo? Charlie wondered. *Brooke lost her beauty, but what could it take from him? His relationship with his father? Maybe... but that was already lost, wasn't it? What else could it be?*

"ANSWER!" the Smith demanded.

"I do," Theodore said softly. "I agree to sacrifice."

"Don't do it!" Charlie screamed – or *tried* to – but the paralysis in his throat only allowed the first word to escape his lips.

"Too LATE," the Smith said. It leaned back its bulbous head, parted its wide, rubbery lips, filled its throat to bursting point and then let out an enormous "*CROOOOAK!*"

The whole cavern echoed with its thunder.

Theodore looked around, wild-eyed. "What's happening?" he gasped, checking himself out in the reflection of the crystal. "Am I changing? Am I turning into something?" Then, panicked, "Do I look *green*?"

Violet shook her head. "No. I don't see anything yet."

Yet.

The cavern was silent and still. The Smith stood there quietly, betraying nothing.

"C'mon, what?" Theodore shouted. "What did you do to me? The waiting is worse than the result!"

"No, it's not," Brooke moaned. "Trust me." And that was when they heard the cackle.

Manic and definitely female, it drew closer with surprising speed. Soon Charlie could make out another sound – the frenzied beating of wings. Within moments, that horrible, shrill laughter was so loud that everyone instinctively clamped their hands over their ears – everyone but Charlie because his arms wouldn't obey. There was something familiar about that cackle and it took him only a moment to recognise where he had heard it before.

It can't be… Charlie thought. *Not now. Not* her…

The Hag Queen soared into the chamber on wide, leathery wings. Her pink ballgown was filthy and tattered. A tarnished tiara rested atop the stringy hair that hung round her face and her long, hooked nose nearly touched the warty protrusion of her chin. She grinned, her mouth a forest of teeth.

"You called?"

The giant frog nodded. "I have a little TREAT for you."

"It had better be good. You interrupted me while I was feeding my Gorgons. The poor dears never get to eat any of the humans that get lost in their maze because they always turn them to stone before they *can*." She sighed dramatically. "Of course, it's not the *monsters'* fault. As soon as a human so much as glances at them—" the Hag snapped her fingers "—it's statue time. And to make matters *worse*, people are constantly coming in and trying to decapitate my snaky-headed little darlings in order to revive their friends. I mean, really! It's absolutely *brutal* being a monster these days. Don't you agree?"

The Smith grunted. "ENOUGH chatter. I called you here, HAG, because I have a JOB for you. Something you might – *crooooak!* – ENJOY."

The Hag Queen glanced at Charlie and his friends. "Oh, *them* again? Not long ago, they paid me a visit – along with that delightful cowboy." She licked her black lips and then pranced forward, as if she were as thin and delicate as a ballerina. "So which one of these tasty little morsels may I dine on? Or, wait! Do I get to *choose*? Yes, that's it! Delicious… delicious…"

She pointed at each child in turn with a crusty fingernail. Charlie noticed that there were too many knuckles on her finger – as many as five. "Eeeny, meeny, miny, mo… drain a human, let it go! Or maybe I *don't* let it go! Maybe I just drain the miserable thing and then eat it all up! I mean, *look* at me – I'm positively wasting away…" She rubbed the rolls of fat on her belly.

"ENOUGH," the Smith said, leaping forward. "There's only ONE child available to you today. THIS one."

He nodded towards Theodore. The Hag Queen surveyed the boy with an arched eyebrow, clearly disappointed.

"He's such a little fish – and he's all bones. Why not just give him to me and let me fatten him up a bit?"

"NO. He must stay here and you must take his sacrifice NOW."

She stuck out her bottom lip in a mock pout. "Spoilsport!" Then, with a gentle flutter of her wings, she flew to Theodore. "Why don't you tell that mean old frog to leave us alone so you can come and play with me, sweetie? Would you like that? Would you like to live in my glorious mansion, your every need attended to by my Ladies-in-Hating?" She batted her eyes at him flirtatiously. "Hmmm, child?"

"I, uh…" Theodore's voice was raspy with revulsion. "I don't think so, ma'am. In fact, I'm going to say that's a definite NW – no way."

The Hag's eyes hardened. "Too bad." She turned back to the Smith. "So what's it to be then? Which memories am I to drain from the child? Tell me quick – he bores me."

The Smith grinned. "Then perhaps this will interest you. You will take away every last vestige of his FRIENDSHIP with the boy known as Charlie Benjamin."

"No…" Theodore gasped.

No! Charlie thought. *Not that!*

The Smith continued. "You will drink deeply of every experience they have ever HAD, every – *crooooak!* – moment they have ever shared. Charlie Benjamin is the most important thing in his life and now he will SACRIFICE their friendship."

"You can't do that to him…" Violet said.

Definitely not! Charlie thought, although he couldn't say it out loud. *Don't, Theodore. Don't let her do this…*

Theodore backed away from the Hag Queen, panic rising in his eyes. "Please, pick something else. *Anything* else."

The Hag became excited. "Yes! Look how it frightens him! These memories must mean a great deal to the child… Ooooh, just think how they'll taste!" She began to drool. "Mmmmmm, delicious! Delightful! *Delectable*, even!" Her black tongue flickered in and out and she eagerly licked her fingers. "Oh, my! I will drink all his tasty memories, yes, indeed – *every last drop* – and when I am done, the boy will no longer even be able to remember Charlie Benjamin's *name*…"

She snatched Theodore up in her strong arms, then enfolded him in her wings and unfurled her tongue to its full, horrible length – it whipped through the air like a putrid worm.

"Say goodbye to Charlie…" she cackled.

"Forget this," Violet said. Raising her axe high, she reached out and snatched the Hag's tongue, preparing to chop it off at the root.

"Wait!" Theodore shouted.

Violet paused, her body thrumming with rage. Theodore continued.

"You can't stop this, Violet. At least you *shouldn't*. Brooke has already suffered and so will you. We've all got to do this to give Charlie a chance – because if *he* doesn't have one, *no one* does."

Violet considered. "I really don't care."

She chopped off the Hag's tongue. In a fountain of black ichor, the meaty, severed tube dropped to the ground, where it spasmed and writhed like a python.

Well, that's that, Charlie thought.

Even though he was thrilled to see his friend spared the terrible kiss of the Hag, that thought was soon pushed aside by another – one more darkly practical.

If Theodore doesn't sacrifice this, how in the world are we ever going to get the sword?

Suddenly, to everyone's horror, the nub of tongue that remained in the Hag's mouth began to grow, shooting from between her scaly lips like fishing line playing out. Within moments, it was the same length as before.

"No more games!" the Hag Queen screeched and Charlie was surprised by the fierceness in her voice – usually, she liked to toy with people more. "No more bargains. No more delays. It's time to feast."

Theodore turned to Charlie then, fighting back tears. "Goodbye, DT. You were my best friend. Seriously. Remember that."

And before Charlie could let Theodore know that the feeling was mutual, the Hag plunged her hideous tongue deep into his friend's ear – down, down, into his brain – and began to suck. Memories rushed away from Theodore, like an express train leaving a station, and he savoured each one in the fleeting seconds before it was gone.

The first time he and Charlie had met, high up in the pirate ship at the very top of the Nightmare Academy. How lost Charlie had looked then, sitting quietly on the worn, wooden bench. How very *alone*. Theodore had known instantly that the two of them would become friends. That it was, somehow… inevitable. He had never made friends easily – most people considered him far too strange – but in Charlie, he had finally, after all these years, found a soulmate.

As soon as Theodore thought it, the memory was gone, followed by another one – this one tied closely to a single emotion. *Pride*.

The pride Theodore felt on the beach at the Nightmare Academy, as he shared with Charlie the details of the extraordinary courage and quick thinking he had displayed during Slagguron's terrible attack on the great tree. His portals had saved Mama Rose, along with countless other students, from the rampage of that foul worm. That was the day he had come into his own as a Nethermancer, the day he had finally embraced that great and difficult art, and the pride he had felt from his accomplishment was unparalleled. Charlie had been genuinely thrilled for his friend's success and, to Theodore, that had meant, well, *everything*.

Gone.

The Hag sucked it away and stored it in her monstrous brain along with all his other memories of Charlie – the tears of failure and the shouts of laughter during moments of great happiness, all the frustrations and the joys and the tragedies and triumphs that make up the intricate fabric of any true friendship.

All gone now.

Stolen – by a monster – to give a friend Theodore could no longer even remember a chance to save the world. The Hag Queen let him go then, sucking that long tongue back into her mouth. She licked her lips in something like ecstasy. "Yes! Good! Wonderful, in fact! Tasty! Tasty! TASTY!"

Theodore crumpled to the ground and Violet rushed to his side. She held the trembling boy, who stared up at her in confusion.

"Where am I?" he asked.

She wiped a tear from her eye and did her best to smile comfortingly. "With friends."

"Really?" He looked around, glassy-eyed. "I don't recognise anyone."

"Not even me?"

He shook his head. "I don't think so. Maybe... You look *sort* of familiar, but it's hard to..." He focused intently on her, clearly struggling to figure out where he might know her from. Then he finally gave up and shrugged. "Not sure. Sorry. Have we met?"

"We have."

"Huh. Weird." Theodore turned to Charlie with a quizzical look in his eyes. "And you – I don't recognise you at all. Do I know you?"

It took all of Charlie's effort to break through the paralysis from the Shock Wasp and reply, although he could only manage one small word: "No."

Just saying it made him sick – but what other option did he have? Why torment his friend? Why make him struggle to recall memories and connections that were now lost? Charlie was sure that no was the right answer... and yet it broke his heart to say it.

Theodore nodded. "Yeah, didn't think so. Too bad. You're definitely missing out. I'm actually pretty spectacular." He rose shakily to his feet. "So can I go home now? I think I need to get back to the Academy. They're going to be declaring us Banishers or Nethermancers pretty soon and I definitely don't want to miss that. I'm going to be a Banisher obviously, just like my dad. He's one of the greatest Banishers of all time, you know – just like the rest of my family. I mean, that's just a *fact*. Hey, maybe you can meet him sometime!"

Violet nodded. "Sure. Maybe we can."

"Excellent!"

The Smith stepped towards the Hag. "It is done. The boy has SACRIFICED. BEGONE."

"With pleasure." She turned to Theodore and smiled ghoulishly. "Goodbye, sweetie. And if you ever want to come and visit a gorgeous little cupcake like myself, my offer still stands. We can have *such fun* together." She blew him a kiss – it smelled like rotten meat – then flew away with a cackle.

There was silence then, a sense of impending doom. Charlie knew what was coming next, they *all* did, and he dreaded it to his core. Finally, the Smith turned to Violet and asked his question.

"Do YOU, Violet Sweet, agree to SACRIFICE that which is most important to you so that Charlie Benjamin can wield the SWORD?"

Violet, tired and alone, gave her answer.

CHAPTER ELEVEN
A RELUCTANT REUNION

Deep inside the Nightmare Academy, the Headmaster's study was quiet and still. A small, bird-like Snark nibbled away at a wooden railing. Suddenly, it looked up, alarmed, as a fiery portal burst open in the centre of the room, filling it with light and heat. Tabitha Greenstreet rushed through, followed by Rex, who carried the Headmaster in his strong arms.

"Place me on the couch, Mr Henderson," she commanded, gesturing to a worn bamboo sofa covered in a dark, wine-coloured fabric.

"I can bring you up to your bed if you'd be more comfor—"

"The *couch*," she repeated sternly, "will be just fine."

Rex gently set the Headmaster down, careful not to aggravate her wounds. "You hungry? You need anything from the galley? Biscuits or something?"

She shook her head. "What I need is for you to check on my *students* and make sure they are safe from the wrath of those infernal Elemental Golems."

"Right away," Tabitha said with a nod. "But let me portal you somewhere else while we do it. The Nightmare Division will be looking for you here. We're still in exile, you know."

The Headmaster waved away her concern. "The day I start worrying about Director Drake's insane 'orders' is the day I resign as Headmaster." She sighed wearily. "I only wish I knew how Mr Benjamin and his friends were faring…"

"Tabby and I can go check up on 'em," Rex said. "Maybe we can give 'em a hand. We'd love to do it."

"I know you would, Rexford. But unfortunately, the threat they are facing is from something dying inside themselves – something precious and irreplaceable. It is not from a monster we can slay."

And that was when they heard the voice – so deep and loud that the entire tree shook with its thunder.

"YOUNG MR BENJAMIN! Come out here, boy! Come and talk to your old friend!"

Rex and Tabitha glanced at each other.

"Can't be…" the cowboy said.

They raced to the balcony off the Headmaster's study and looked out on to the beach beyond the great tree. Something was standing there near the crashing waves, something huge and monstrous.

"Pinch?" Rex asked, staring in dismay. "That you?"

The gigantic antlike creature nodded. His enormous legs, as thick as the Academy's lower branches, were dug into the white sand beneath him like pilings supporting a pier. "Yes, it is me. Surprised?"

"A little. I mean, you were never the most attractive son-of-a-gun on the planet, but now you're takin' ugly to a whole new level."

"Beauty is in the eye of the beholder, Rexford. I happen to think I'm quite the catch. That is, if you *could* catch me – which you can't. No mere human can any more. Certainly not *these* fools, although they tried."

Pinch opened his massive fists, allowing the corpses of several Banishers to tumble to the soft sand like rag dolls.

Rex grimaced – even after the deaths he'd dealt in his life, he still hated to see it. "Where did they come from?"

"The Netherforge. I went there to look for our mutual friend, Charlie Benjamin, but unfortunately, he was not present."

That's probably because he's still in the Chamber of Ancient

Weapons, Rex thought darkly, *trying to get the sword.*

"Well, it's a dang shame you didn't get to meet up with him," the cowboy replied. "Anything I can help you with? Or did you come here just to reminisce about the good old days?"

"I wasn't aware there were any." Pinch stepped forward. "I thought, perhaps, that Charlie Benjamin might be here with you."

"Sorry, Pinch. Ain't seen him. Hey, have you tried calling Directory Ant-sistance? Maybe they could help."

"*Ant*-sistance? Is that an ant joke?"

"Yeah, but you ain't laughing, so I guess it wasn't a very good one."

Pinch took another step forward. "You will either bring young Mr Benjamin here to me or I will tear every ship from the Academy's branches until I find him."

"Now I don't know why we gotta resort to *violence*. I mean, why can't we just talk this out like two grown men – you know, man-to-mant?"

"Mant? Another ant joke?"

"Yeah, but that was a pretty good one, I think."

Pinch smiled. "Do you? So will you assist me, Rexford – or shall I simply kill you now?"

Rex raised a finger. "Just hold that thought." He turned to Tabitha and whispered, "Well, darlin', looks like this is the end of the road. Now here's what you're gonna do – go get the Headmaster and start portalling everyone outta here."

"You want to run?" she whispered. "Let's stay and fight."

"Fight? You see what Pinch looks like now? He's the size of a building and crazy to boot. No fighting's gonna happen here – only dying – and if we try it, we're gonna take a lot of students with us. I can't chance that." He turned back to Pinch and shouted: "OK, I made my decision. I'm gonna go with option two – the one where you 'kill me now'."

Rex threw his lasso up to the prow of the wrecked ship above him and swung out on it – straight at Pinch – like Tarzan on a vine. Pinch snatched him from the air with a giant claw.

"Rex!" Tabitha yelled. "What in the world are you doing?"

"What I need to, just like *you* need to do what I told ya to!" Rex turned back to Pinch – this close, his red, plated face loomed like the side of a skyscraper. "OK, Ugly, you got me. Now go ahead and do what you promised – kill me now. Go on. Squeeze me to death. Pop off my head like a cork – shouldn't take but a second."

"What are you up to, Rexford?" Pinch asked, eyes narrowing.

"Up to? Dang, Pinch, you always think everyone's got an ulterior motive just cos *you* always got one. Now go on and squeeze. Here, I'll give you a count – one, two, three, *squeeze!*"

"*Stop that!*"

"What?" Rex looked genuinely befuddled. "What's the problem now?"

"You're trying to control things. I'm the one in charge here – not you!"

"Geez, *obviously* you're in charge, Pinch. I mean, you're the killer here – I'm just the killee. Now here we go: one, two, three, *squeeze!*"

"I said STOP IT!"

"Or what? You'll kill me?"

Pinch groaned. "You are the single most frustrating human being in existence, do you know that?"

Rex grinned. "Guilty as charged. Just ask Tabitha. She'll go on and on about it."

I'll be danged, Rex thought. *This crazy plan is actually* working.

He knew that Pinch wanted – more than anything – to be the most powerful one around. As long as he kept insisting that Pinch kill him right away, Rex was pretty sure that the vain man would refuse. After all, no one could tell Edward Pinch what to do! It wasn't a great plan, but Rex hoped that, with a little luck, it would at least give Tabitha enough time to evacuate the students from the Academy before Pinch could turn his full fury on them.

"Let's just get back to the business at hand," the cowboy said, "which is the killing of little old me. Now you just do exactly what I tell you, Pinch. On the count of three – squeeze. Here we go. One, two, three – *squeeze*!"

Then, to Rex's horror, Pinch did.

Deep in the Chamber of Ancient Weapons, Violet turned to the Smith.

"Whatever the sacrifice is, I accept it so that Charlie can get the sword."

"EXCELLENT."

The giant frog's eyes glittered and Charlie, still paralysed, was repulsed to see how thrilled the creature was to inflict more pain.

How many other seekers have there been? he wondered. *And how much did their friends suffer at the whim of the Smith?* Given the extraordinary toll taken on the people involved, Charlie thought it would have been a miracle if *anyone* had ever actually laid hands on the priceless weapon.

Of course, it wasn't actually *priceless* – it had a price. A terrible one.

"Brooke BRIGHTON," the Smith said, turning to the girl. "I require you to open a PORTAL."

She snorted angrily. "Why would I – *crooooak!* – ever help you?"

"Because if you do NOT, then your sacrifice will be in vain and Charlie Benjamin will not get the sword!"

"Ask Theodore to open one – he's better at it than me."

"Not any more," the Smith replied with a sneer. "Now open a portal, girl – to the Nightmare Division!"

Gritting her teeth, she did. A purple portal snapped open into the heart of the High Council chamber, startling several employees working there.

"YOU!" the Smith yelled, pointing a warty finger at a man in an orange jumpsuit as he mopped the floor. "Get General Dagget here now. Tell him the SMITH is ready with – *crooooak!* – the SACRIFICE."

The sacrifice. Charlie suddenly realised what the Smith intended to do and his heart sank. He wondered if Violet suspected as well and he could see from her grim expression that she did.

Within moments, General Dagget rushed through the portal, followed by two Banishers from the Nightmare Division. The tall man glanced around, quickly assessing the situation. His gaze settling on Brooke's horrible disfigurement. He struggled to conceal his revulsion.

"I see the girl has sacrificed."

"Yes, 'the girl' has sacrificed," Brooke said, moving towards him. "And thanks for calling me 'the girl' and not something more appropriate like 'the frog'."

William grunted dismissively. He turned to Theodore. "Are you OK, son?"

"Definitely. What's up, Dad? Cool outfit! Nice medals." His eyes widened in surprise. "Wow – when did you make General?"

William surveyed him with clinical detachment then turned to the Smith. "Has my son sacrificed as well?"

The Smith nodded. "He has lost all memory of the boy who was once most – *crooooak!* – IMPORTANT to him."

William seemed relieved. "Good. Time will show it's for the best." He flashed Charlie an angry glance. "The boy he once knew has brought him nothing but pain. He is better left forgotten."

"Who are you talking about?" Theodore asked.

"No one, son."

No one.

Maybe it is *for the best*, Charlie thought. *Maybe William was right*. Theodore would probably be happier now that Charlie was no longer a part of his life. He would certainly be *safer*. Heck, they all would be.

"You may now take the GIRL, General," the Smith said, gesturing to Violet. "She has agreed to SACRIFICE the thing most valuable to her… and that is her BANISHING ability. She must – *crooooak!* – be REDUCED."

The word hung in the air with terrible finality. For months, Director Drake had screamed for their Reduction and yet they had always managed to escape the barbaric procedure – but now the war against the monsters of the Nether, as well as the safety of the entire planet, seemed to depend on Violet sacrificing herself to the very thing they had struggled so hard to avoid.

"*You* might call it a sacrifice," William said to the giant frog, "but, at the Nightmare Division, we simply call it justice. The girl chose exile, which banned her from getting involved in the Monster War under penalty of Reduction." He gestured to the Sword of Sacrifice as it glittered in the amber crystal. "I'd call this getting pretty involved, wouldn't you?"

"Yeah," Violet said with a huff. "Trying to save the world. What a crime."

"There's a right way to do things, young lady, and a wrong way. You chose *wrong*."

"I stood up for my friends. I protected them. When

have you ever protected anyone but yourself?"

William grimaced. "It's all black and white to you, isn't it? That's youth talking. When you get older, you'll realise the world is not so simple."

"That's only because of people like you and the Director."

"ENOUGH of this babbling," the Smith croaked. "It is TIME. Take her now."

No, Charlie thought. *Please… no…*

"For what it's worth," William said to Violet with just the slightest hint of compassion, "the procedure is completely painless. When it's over, you won't even know what you've lost."

"Like Theodore?"

"Yes, in fact. Theodore is *happy* now that he doesn't have the temptations and distractions of that 'other' one rolling around in his head." He turned to his son. "Aren't you?"

Theodore shrugged. "I guess so."

"Soon you will be certain." The General squeezed his son's shoulder reassuringly with a large, calloused hand.

Violet shook her head in something like amazement.

"Wow. I keep expecting you to reveal some hidden agenda to explain why you're being so horrible. I mean, after all, you're Theodore's *father* – you can't *really* be this way, can you? But you *are*. There's no secret, noble reason you're acting like this. You're just a really bad guy."

"I understand that you're upset. At your age, I probably would have been as well. You may find this hard to believe, but I have Banished all my life and the ability has brought me nothing but pain. Be thankful you're soon going to be rid of it."

"You'll forgive me if I don't send a thank-you note."

Charlie continued to be amazed by how strong and determined Violet had become. It was hard to reconcile the girl in front of him with the Violet he had met just six short months ago – the Violet who only wanted to draw dragons and be left in peace. She was a dragon herself now.

"So how are we going to do this?" William asked. "The easy way… or the hard?"

Violet glared at him. "When have I ever done anything the easy way?" She swung her axe at the General.

William, startled by the suddenness of the attack, barely managed to sidestep the blow, falling to one knee. With practised grace, he drew his sword and parried her second strike, while the other two Banishers behind him rushed at Violet, tackling her.

"What are you doing?" Theodore shouted. "Don't hurt her!"

"She won't be hurt," William replied, "if she *stops fighting*!"

It took all three adults almost a minute to wrench the axe from Violet's hands and bind her arms behind her. Finally, she stopped struggling. "I'm not going to fight any more. I'm done. I just wanted to make you work for it."

William pulled her to her feet. "I respect that. Truly." He handed her to the Banishers. "Now take her to the Division and tell the doctors to begin the procedure immediately. And be *careful*. She bites."

The Banishers nodded. They each grabbed an arm and pulled Violet towards the open portal.

"See you, Charlie," she said, looking back over her shoulder. "You get that sword and you get this done, you hear me? You kill the Fifth for me."

"I will," Charlie whispered, his heart breaking.

The Banishers pulled Violet roughly into the Nightmare Division and out of sight.

CHAPTER TWELVE
THE FINAL TURN IS TAKEN

Charlie began to feel his arms and legs again as the paralysis wore off. They burned as if stung by hornets.

That's nothing compared to what Violet is about to go through, he thought. *Bring on the pain. I deserve it.*

Rex had been right – the quest for the sword required suffering, far more than he had ever imagined necessary. But was it all worth it? While Charlie contemplated the depth of his debt to his friends, Theodore, whose sacrifice made him falsely believe that he was friendless, turned to his father.

"I want to go with you. I don't really know anyone here. Can I come to the Division too?"

William seemed pleased by his son's request. "Of course."

"Take the GIRL as well," the Smith said, nodding to Brooke. "Her part in this is FINISHED."

"Gladly." William pointed his longsword at Charlie and then added, almost casually, "And I will be taking Charlie Benjamin with me too."

"WHAT?" The Smith seemed genuinely surprised. "The boy is under MY watch now. He seeks the SWORD."

"He is a *fugitive* who has breached the terms of his exile. By order of Director Drake, he is to be Reduced along with the girl."

"What you and DIRECTOR DRAKE do with Charlie Benjamin AFTER he leaves my protection is of no CONCERN to me!" the Smith thundered. "You can – *crooooak!* – boil his bones for all I care. But for now, the boy is MINE."

William stepped towards the frog. The air grew electric with danger. "Be careful, Smith," the General said, raising his two-handed sword. "You once helped me create this weapon and, for that, I am grateful to you… but not enough to stop me from using it to chop off your slimy head."

"You mean before I TOUCH you?"

William cast a nervous look at Brooke's ruined face.

She smiled back at him. "Go on, piss off the frog. You'll – *crooooak!* – love the result, trust me."

The Banisher looked as though he wanted to reply, but finally thought better of it. He turned to Charlie. "We'll meet again. You can't escape your judgement for ever." Then he strode towards the portal, gesturing for Brooke and Theodore to follow. "Come."

"Goodbye, Charlie…" Brooke said, looking at him one last time. "And good luck." She stepped through the portal.

Theodore, lagging a couple of steps behind, turned back to Charlie. "My name's Theodore by the way. Last name Dagget. Not Dagger, Dagget, with a *t*." He smiled. "I know it may seem kind of crazy, but I've got a good feeling about you. I think we're going to be best friends."

Theodore nodded firmly as if that sealed the deal, then he strode through the portal and into the Nightmare Division. Moments later, the portal closed behind him, leaving Charlie Benjamin alone with the Smith.

"It is DONE," the creature growled. "Your friends have – *crooooak!* – stood TRUE. You are LUCKY."

I don't feel lucky, Charlie thought. *I feel like someone who has just cost his best friends the most important things in their lives.*

The pain in his arms and legs was beginning to subside a little. He couldn't move yet – not much, anyway – but he was definitely feeling a little better and he thought it wouldn't be too long before movement was possible.

The Smith hopped over to the giant crystal in the very centre of the cavern that housed the sword. Closing its eyes tightly, the creature stroked the gleaming facets of the gem, mumbling darkly – Charlie couldn't make out what exactly. As the Smith's muttering intensified, light began to pour from the crystal. Then, with a loud *crack*, it fractured down the centre and shattered into a thousand pieces. The sword remained in the air, turquoise light illuminating it from within.

"The Sword of Sacrifice is YOURS, boy!" the Smith said. "Come and CLAIM it!"

Rex had gambled with his life and lost.

As the crushing pressure from Pinch's fist built on his body, the cowboy could dimly see bright, purple flashes throughout the Academy.

Portals, he thought as he began to drift into unconsciousness.

Kids are escaping, but how many?

And did the Headmaster get out with them?

And how about Tabitha?

And then he had another, stranger thought.

Why do I have enough time to think *all these thoughts? Shouldn't I be dead already?*

And that was when he noticed something odd happening to Pinch's head. One side of it was collapsing, like a giant balloon deflating. In fact, Pinch's entire body appeared to be folding in on itself – his massive chest caved in as his long, antlike legs buckled and then crumpled to the ground.

"What's happening?" Pinch growled as the brilliant red colour leached from his skin. His right fist continued to shrink along with the rest of him and soon Pinch could hold Rex no more. With a shout, the cowboy plummeted through the air and slammed into the soft, warm sand. Grunting with effort, he struggled to his feet and turned to discover that he was now standing next to a small, dazed, thirteen-year-old boy.

Pinch had reverted to his previous form.

"Well, ain't *this* a pleasant surprise..." Rex said, grinning.

The fear in Pinch's eyes was unmistakable. Without a word, he backed away, snapping open an escape portal behind him.

"Whoa, whoa, whoa!" Rex continued in his best, calming voice. "No need to rush off. Now I know we've had our differences, what with you just tryin' to kill me and all, but I say let bygones be bygones. You ain't a monster, Pinch – you're just a *fella*, like me. Let's start fresh."

Pinch shook his head. "How stupid do you think I am? That's a trick, Rexford. I know you too well."

"Honest to goodness," Rex said, putting his hand over his heart. "Look, it ain't exactly like we're blameless on our end. I mean, everyone in the Nightmare Division hates us – heck, they got us in exile. See, we're renegades, just like you. Now let's stop this silliness and band together." Rex nodded to the Nightmare Academy. "Tabitha is with the Headmaster in her study right now. What say you and me go up there together and we hash this thing out like men?"

Rex offered his hand. Pinch stared at it with something close to longing.

"Pinch," Rex said kindly. "You ain't a monster. You're *family*. Come join us."

For a moment, Rex actually thought that Pinch might take his hand – but then a darkness passed over the bitter man's face.

"Never!" he shouted, then turned and leaped through the portal and into the Nether.

"The boy still *lives*?" the Queen of Nightmares shrieked, her voice echoing down the shiny spirals of the massive shell she called home. "If he lives, then you have failed! You miserable, weak, filthy HUMAN!"

Pinch couldn't help but tremble in the face of her terrible fury. The few Nethercreatures remaining in the throne room quickly scuttled away to escape her wrath.

"I beg your forgiveness," Pinch pleaded. "I thought I had found Benjamin at the Nightmare Academy but, before I could confirm it, I changed back to…. this." He gestured to his own frail body with disgust. "A miserable, weak, filthy human – like you just said."

The Queen of Nightmares strode towards him on her long, red legs. Her silver hair flashed on her head like a crown. "Do not presume to think you can appease me with your grovelling! I gave you a gift, a magnificent new body, and yet you failed to use it to do the one simple thing I asked of you! Kill the boy, I said! And you did NOT!"

Pinch kept his head bowed low. "I have no excuse…"

"Of course you don't! Do you think it is easy to do what I do? I have summoned enough Golems to tear this planet apart, and each time I summon one, it exacts upon me a horrific price! I have grown *weak* from my destruction and I ask only that you kill *one boy* while I conquer an entire world! My dark deeds have not spared me even a moment to replenish myself from the Slumber and yet you fail me in the most basic—"

Then, to Pinch's shock, the Queen of Nightmares stumbled to one knee.

Half a world away, in Australia, a Water Golem tearing apart the magnificent clamshell façade of the Sydney Opera House exploded in a massive spray. As people watched in horror, it rained back down into the waves along Bennelong Point. Back in the heart of the giant nautilus shell, the Queen looked up at Pinch with venom in her eyes. "There! Are you *happy*! I have just lost a Golem because of you! I don't have enough strength to maintain the hundreds that I have created *and* keep the fires of my fury burning – a fury that is due solely to your miserable, human incompetence!"

"I will not fail you again," Pinch said, desperate to calm her. "Before I lost my monstrous form, I was at the Nightmare Academy. I thought Benjamin might have returned there to reunite with the Headmaster. He values her counsel and they're both Double-Threats, so I thought—"

"What did you say?" the Queen interrupted. "*Who* is a Double-Threat along with the boy?"

Pinch seemed taken aback by the question. "The Headmaster of the Nightmare Academy. In fact, she's one of the most powerful—"

"Take me to her."

"Right now?" Pinch asked, his voice trembling.

"This instant. I've no time to lose."

"Of course, my lady."

With a shaking hand, Pinch opened a portal.

The walk across the cavern that held the Sword of Sacrifice was torturous, but Charlie forced his protesting body to obey. It was like moving through tar and his arms and legs felt as if they were being pierced with steel needles. Although the pain was immense, he knew it was nothing compared to what his friends had given up to allow him to make this epic journey of twenty steps.

"GRASP it!" the Smith said as soon as Charlie was within reach of the weapon. "Make it your OWN! WIELD it!"

Charlie reached out... and grabbed the sword.

As soon as he touched it, its power thrummed through him and his entire body felt like a live wire conducting a current. The pain of the paralysis disappeared and was replaced by a feeling of strength – strength and confidence. Charlie held the sword aloft and was surprised to discover that it seemed to weigh no more than a grain of sand.

"You feel POWERFUL?" the Smith asked.

Charlie nodded.

"You feel – *crooooak!* – INVINCIBLE?"

"Yes."

Charlie waved the sword through the air – tentatively at first, then with more vigour. Turquoise sparks trailed behind it like fireworks.

"Yes, I do! I feel... unstoppable. I feel like I can take on the world!"

The Smith grinned with dark delight.

"You must have PATIENCE, boy. The sword is GLORIOUS, yes, but it is not yet CHARGED. You must bring it to the Netherforge, boy. Plunge it into the well in the centre, where the MAGMA bubbles, so that it can – *crooooak!* – draw power from the CORE! Only THEN will it be strong enough to SLAY the FIFTH! Go NOW, boy! Go to the FORGE."

To the creature's great surprise, Charlie shook his head. "Maybe later. I have something else I have to do first."

"WHAT? What could be MORE important than destroying the creature that's destroying your WORLD?"

"Saving my friends. Saving Violet before she's Reduced." Charlie grimaced. "Before I'm done, everyone's going to get what's coming to them."

He opened a portal into the Nightmare Division.

"Beware…" the Smith croaked. "Vengeance is a DISEASE. It will ROT you. It will RUIN you."

Charlie shrugged. "Maybe. But there's another disease that's been infecting the Nightmare Division and I'm going to get rid of it before it destroys us all." He stared into the portal, his sword gleaming. "It's time for Director Drake to get a taste of his own medicine. And once I'm done with him, I'm going to pay a little visit to the Fifth."

Then Charlie stepped through the portal and into the Inner Chamber of the Nightmare Division, into the place where his friend, Violet, was about to be subjected to horror beyond imagining – unless he could stop it in time.

He didn't plan to fail.

"Finish portalling out the rest of the students," the Headmaster said to Tabitha from the couch in her study. "Pinch may well return and we cannot take that chance."

Almost as soon as she had finished speaking, a portal snapped open next to Tabitha and the Queen of Nightmares strode through, followed by Pinch.

"Talk of the devil," Rex muttered.

The Headmaster struggled to rise to a sitting position. "What is the meaning of this?"

Without even waiting for a reply, Rex drew his short sword and leaped at the intruders. Before he was able to get to them, the Queen of Nightmares reached out and touched him gently on the forehead. Rex collapsed to the ground.

Tabitha raised her hand, preparing to open a portal underneath their attackers, but she never got that far. The Queen touched her on the shoulder and the Nethermancer dropped to the worn, wooden floor of the ship, unconscious.

The Headmaster, struggling to her feet, glared at Pinch and said only one word – "traitor" – before being brushed by the Queen and falling into a coma-like sleep herself.

After surveying all three humans, who lay at her feet like bewitched characters from a fairy tale, the Queen of Nightmares closed her eyes and smiled. "It is good. They are powerful – particularly the old one. I can already feel them re-energising me inside the Slumber."

"What is the Slumber?" Pinch asked, staring at his former colleagues in quiet amazement.

The Queen of Nightmares grinned. "Cross me one day, Edward… and you may well find out." She opened her eyes and turned to him. "But that will not happen. You have pleased me."

"Thank you."

"And, as your reward, you may now grow strong again." She sliced open a finger   and green blood began to flow.

"Drink," she said. "Drink and become mighty, and then bring me the head of the *boy*."

"I will. And I will not fail you this time. I will find him and destroy him. I *promise*."

Pinch leaned down… and began to drink.

PART THREE
THE POISONOUS PLOT
OF DIRECTOR DRAKE

CHAPTER THIRTEEN
THE FIGHT BEGINS

The Nightmare Division had never seemed so unwelcoming.

Charlie Benjamin strode into the hallway, his shining new weapon clasped tightly in his right hand. Motion detectors and digital cameras kept silent, electronic watch over every centimetre of the highly classified facility. The air was chill and constantly scrubbed by large, humming machines – presumably to keep the ever-present computers functioning at optimum capacity – and a faint smell of antiseptic filled the air.

Charlie dimly remembered the first time he had visited this place, how overwhelmed he had been by the bigness and *strangeness* of it all – the monsters in cages wheeled down hallways by bustling workers in their colour-coordinated jumpsuits, the unusual signs on the doors ('Gnome De-Juicing Facility' stuck in his head for some odd reason). It had been a lot to absorb, but it had also been incredibly exciting.

Not any more.

What once had been exhilarating now just felt alien and ominous. Of course, like everyone, he had heard stories of how wonderful the Division used to be under the guidance of Director Goodnight, how vibrant and full of purpose it was. The Nethermancers, Banishers and Facilitators who worked for him many years ago had truly felt that they were united in their mission to save the world.

But that feeling was long gone. Under Director Drake, the people currently employed at the Division seemed sad and defeated, their Gifts marginalised by a man who secretly despised them because he did not have those Gifts himself. A blanket of fear covered the whole place like a funeral shroud.

It's a real shame, Charlie thought. *Who knows, maybe someday the Division can be restored to its former glory...*

It was a good thought, a *noble* one in fact, but he knew its realisation would have to wait for some distant future. The present demanded hard choices and tough action if he was going to save Violet – which he had every intention of doing.

"You there!" yelled a beefy Banisher walking towards Charlie. "I recognise you – you're Charlie Benjamin! You're not allowed here!"

"Where's the Reduction Room?" Charlie asked, not breaking stride.

"Did you hear what I just said? I'm placing you under arrest by order of Director Drake!" The Banisher raised his thick metal club. "Don't make me use this on you, young—"

Charlie swung the Sword of Sacrifice at the Banisher's weapon, shattering it. The Banisher looked down at his ruined club, astonished.

"How did you—?"

"Where is the Reduction Room?" Charlie repeated.

The Banisher shifted uncertainly. "See, the point is I'm not really allowed to—"

"Tell me. *Now.*"

The man looked deeply into Charlie's eyes and saw in them no room for debate or delay. This was not a boy he was dealing with – not any more at least – this was a *man*, a man who was clearly not going to be denied.

Nervously, the Banisher pointed down a hallway. "Straight to the end, then left. It'll be on your right. But if you go down there—"

He never got to finish his sentence because Charlie

brushed past him, running towards the place where he hoped – prayed, in fact – that his friend Violet was being held, untouched and unharmed.

A thick pane of glass provided a clear view of the operating theatre in the Nightmare Division's infamous Reduction Room. Charlie rushed up to it and looked through to see a large, sunken area flooded with intense fluorescent light. Stainless-steel surgical instruments glittered ominously, wielded by doctors in dark red gowns and masks.

Doctors – ha! Charlie thought. *Doctors help you. These horrible people are something else entirely.*

Then he saw her. Violet Sweet lay on an operating table in the very centre of the room, unmoving, unconscious.

Charlie's heart thudded as a doctor in thick-rimmed glasses pointed a shiny metal device at the top of Violet's head. Laser light pulsed from the tip, casting a small, intense dot on her chestnut, brown hair.

"STOP!" Charlie screamed. "VIOLET!" But no one could hear him – the operating room window was bullet- and soundproof.

No problem, Charlie thought, *as long as it's not Ancient-Weapon-of-the-Nether-proof.*

He swung his sword at the thick pane of glass, shattering it. The doctors looked up at him, shocked.

"What are you doing?" the one with the glasses demanded. "Entrance to this room requires an authorisation of Rank 4 or high—"

Charlie opened a portal beneath the man and dropped him, screaming, into the Nether. With a wave of his hand, Charlie snapped the portal shut. "Who's next?" he asked, leaping into the room. The three remaining doctors set down their instruments and began to back away. "Oh, no, no, no," Charlie warned. "Don't you go running off. Wake her up. *Now*."

The doctors glanced at each other uneasily.

"You're too late," a short, squat one said finally. "We finished the procedure just before you arrived."

Charlie wasn't sure he had heard the man correctly. "What... what did you say?"

"The operation is finished," the doctor replied, nervously wiping sweat from his brow. "The patient is... well, she's already been Reduced, you see."

Charlie's mouth went dry. He felt dizzy and gripped the railing beside him to steady himself.

"OK then... just fix it. Just, I don't know, reverse the procedure or whatever it is you do."

The doctor swallowed hard. "I'm sorry. We would

but… it's simply not reversible. Once the operation is done… it's *done*."

"No." Charlie shook his head. "That can't be. It just…" He walked towards Violet's unconscious form. She looked so small there on the metal table, so terribly vulnerable. "You ANIMALS!" he screamed. *"How could you?"*

The doctors quickly backed away from him. Their fear only made Charlie angrier. *Good! You should be afraid*, he thought. *After what you've done, you should all be on your knees, begging forgiveness.*

He advanced on them, his fury rising.

"Charlie Benjamin!"

Charlie recognised the voice instantly. He turned to see Director Drake looking down at him from the shattered window high above, flanked by a full squadron of adult Nethermancers and Banishers. With his grey suit, grey hair and slate-grey eyes, he looked like a charcoal drawing – a figure of a man, minus the humanity.

"Calm down, son," Drake said, his pearly teeth sparkling in the fluorescent light that poured from the operating theatre. "Trust me. It's for the best."

"It's for the best?" Charlie echoed in disbelief. "Violet was my friend and now you… ruined her… and you're telling me it's for the *best*?"

Drake sighed. "Save your indignation for someone who cares. Everything that has happened to her – to *all* of your friends in fact – is entirely *your* fault. After all, if not for you, she would never have been called to sacrifice to the Smith to begin with."

Charlie was aghast – Director Drake's complete indifference to people's suffering was breathtaking. "Why are you doing this to us? All we've ever done is try to help."

"Tell that to the unfortunate Nethermancers and Banishers who perished when you killed the Guardian."

"I didn't kill him. *You* did that! You and General Dagget."

Drake chuckled. "I know you claim we did, but it simply doesn't stand the test of *logic*. Why would the General or I ever do such an unforgivable thing? The death of the Guardian revived the monsters in the lair of the Named which, in turn, caused a bloodbath." He shook his head sadly. "No, there's simply no reason for General Dagget or myself to have committed an atrocity like that. No reason at all."

"There is one," Charlie said, stepping forward. "If the Guardian had lived, the Monster Army would be dead and the Fifth would never have been summoned. If that had happened, then there wouldn't be a need for a

Nightmare Division... or for someone to run it. Someone like *you*."

Charlie could tell from the brief flutter of fear that passed across the Director's face that he had hit a nerve – but Drake quickly recovered.

"The aggression and paranoia you demonstrate is, quite regrettably, common in all Double-Threats, and it often has terrible consequences – the unfortunate case of Edward Pinch has certainly taught us that." The Banishers and Nethermancers behind the Director nodded in agreement – clearly, Double-Threats were not to be trusted. "Pinch went bad," Drake continued smoothly, "and, by accusing me like this, we can now see that you, Mr Benjamin, are sadly well on your way to joining him as a traitor to the human race."

Charlie shook his head. "Someone has to stop you, Drake. Stop you *now*, before you destroy any chance we have of defeating the Fifth."

"Threatening the Director? Tsk, tsk, tsk... Another traitorous thought." Drake plucked a stray thread from his grey suit. "You grow more dangerous by the second, Mr Benjamin. Why not do us all a favour – in fact, do *yourself* one – and lie down on that table next to your little girlfriend. As you can see, the procedure is quick and painless. You will not suffer."

Charlie laughed. "If you actually think I'm going to do that, then you're even crazier than I thought. Everything about you stinks, Drake, and the smell of you makes me want to—"

Charlie stopped. The *smell*. There was something about the smell here that wasn't quite right.

He sniffed carefully, trying to put his finger on it. The operating room was filled with the electric scent of metal, mixed with the tang of antiseptic... but there was another smell too. Something sweet and oddly familiar. This new smell *meant* something, something dangerous. But what was it?

And then Charlie knew. *Cinnamon*.

"You've got to be kidding me," he said and rushed to the surgical sink. He grabbed a beaker of water from it.

"What are you doing?" Director Drake asked, alarmed.

"Yes, what?" Violet added, sitting bolt upright on the operating table, eyes wild with panic.

Charlie smiled darkly. "What are you doing awake? I thought you were unconscious – Mimic." He threw the water in her face.

As soon as it hit, the creature that looked like Violet began to shudder and its skin bubbled and darkened.

Within moments, the outer layer liquefied and drained away into the surgical grate on the floor, revealing a pink, sluglike creature beneath, with no mouth or legs. The monster's arms, however, were long and strong and they each ended in five fingers (*which makes it a Class 5*, Charlie thought instinctively).

Quick as a mongoose, the Mimic reached out and grabbed Charlie by the head – he knew from experience that those powerful hands could instantly crush his skull. With no time to spare, Charlie swung his brightly glowing sword and chopped through the neck of the hideous beast. Its head sailed through the air and splatted against the far wall like an overripe melon.

Charlie looked up at Director Drake.

"Where is she? Where's Violet?"

"I don't know what you think you're—"

"For a Mimic to be able to copy something, its target has to be close by and alive, so *where is she*? Tell me now, unless you want to end up like that!"

Charlie gestured to the decapitated Mimic with his sword. Drake glanced at it queasily.

"She is safe."

"Has she been Reduced?"

No answer from Drake. The bony man dabbed sweat from his upper lip.

"Has she?" Charlie demanded.

Finally, Drake shook his head. "No. She has not."

That doesn't make any sense, Charlie thought. *Why bring her here and not Reduce her? In fact, why even Mimic her to begin with?*

"To answer your unspoken question," another voice said, and Charlie was surprised to see General Dagget walk up behind the Director. "We did all of this for one specific purpose – to lure you here and then capture you."

Charlie's mind reeled. Was this all a trap?

"I know it *seems* complicated, but it's not really," William continued as Brooke and Theodore walked up next to him. "You see, I made a deal with the Director. He agreed that if I could deliver you to him, he would spare your friends from Reduction: Brooke, Violet and, of course, my *son*." William smiled. "And now I have fulfilled my part of the bargain."

Charlie took a step forward, sword raised. "You may have delivered me here, but what makes you think you can *keep* me?"

Just then, right below the shattered viewing window where Drake and the General watched, the lower door to the operating room flew open and Violet – the *real* Violet – burst through. Behind her, Charlie could see two Banishers lying in a broken, crumpled heap.

"She's loose!" one of them shouted, grasping his leg – it jutted out at an odd angle. "Security!"

"Charlie?" Violet yelled. "Portal out! It's a trap – they're just using me to catch you!"

Charlie nodded. "I know – but they don't have me yet."

"Oh, but I'm afraid we *do*," Director Drake said, then turned to the Nethermancer beside him. "Do it NOW."

Purple fire crackled across the woman and, moments later, a wide portal snapped open in the operating room just behind Violet, out of view of everyone but Charlie and the doctors. Charlie glanced into the portal for just a second and immediately knew that he had made a terrible mistake.

Oh, no, he thought. *Gorgons.*

Dozens of the snake-headed monsters hissed from the dark depths of the Gorgon Maze near the mansion of the Hags and, before anyone could react, *Charlie Benjamin was turned to stone*.

CHAPTER FOURTEEN
BAD DAY IN THE GORGON MAZE

"Why did you do that?" Theodore shouted, staring down in shock at the statue of Charlie Benjamin.

"Because we never would have been able to capture him otherwise," William replied. "He's... tricky. But don't worry about it – he won't trouble you any more."

"He didn't trouble me to begin with!"

"That's because you don't remember." William turned and looked his son in the eyes. "This boy caused you a lot of difficulty, Theodore – but I've taken care of everything. You've been forgiven for all of your mistakes and now you don't even have to be burdened with *memories* of the bad times." William smiled and there was something desperate about it. "You and I can start over, son."

Theodore shook his head, confused. "But… he was my friend. Or at least I thought he could be."

"No. He's bad for you. He poisons everything he touches."

"Don't listen to him!" Theodore looked down to see Violet standing in the operating room below. "Charlie was your best friend before and he *still is*!" she yelled. "Come and help me now and I'll prove it!"

"She's lying, son," William said. "She always does."

"*He's* the liar, Theo! Remember what happened in the ice cave, in the lair of the Named? You saw him kill the Guardian! Do you remember? I *know* you can because Charlie wasn't with you at the time, so that memory should still be there."

Theodore tried to remember, but it was difficult. In his mind, the last six months were an unconnected series of snapshots – random pictures assembled out of order and out of context. But then… there it was! He saw an image of his father holding the frail creature known as the Guardian in the icy lair of the Named.

Had that caused its death?

"Come and help me, Theo… join me…" Violet begged.

"Don't listen to her, son. I'm the only one that truly cares about you."

Theodore looked from the pleading eyes of his father to Violet's outstretched hand beckoning him to her, to the marble statue of the boy who looked so terribly familiar, the boy whose friendship seemed almost preordained, as impossible to change as…

Destiny.

"Sorry, Dad," Theodore said. "I have to go."

"Wait! Son!"

Ignoring him, the skinny boy leaped down into the operating room next to Violet. "So what do we do?" he asked.

"Close your eyes and follow me. And don't look at the Gorgons unless you want to end up like Charlie!"

She closed her eyes tightly. Then, with a savage battle cry, Violet leaped through the still-open portal and into the foul stink of the Gorgon Maze. Theodore, shutting his eyes as well, followed.

Moments later, the portal snapped closed behind them, locking them in the Nether.

The brilliantly coloured crystal pathways of the Gorgon Maze branched off in all directions. Gorgons prowled through the labyrinth, carefully weaving around the many statues of humans who had made the mistake of looking directly at them and been turned to stone for their folly.

"OK, so what's the plan?" Theodore asked, feeling around blindly. His hands touched the marble face of a woman who had been trapped lifelessly in the maze longer than he had been alive. "Oh, sorry ..." he muttered. Then, "And now I'm chatting with a statue. Good work, Theodore."

"Just relax," Violet said. "We're here to save Charlie, just like he tried to save me, and we're not going to fail."

"Ah, great! The 'no-fail' plan – exactly the plan I was hoping for. And how are we going to do this exactly?"

"Simple really. We just have to chop off the head of the Gorgon that transformed him – that's the only way to bring Charlie back to life."

"Right. Excellent. So... which one of them did it? Transformed him, I mean."

"Well, how am I supposed to know? And, even if I *did*, I can't exactly look at them now anyway, can I?"

Which was absolutely true – Violet couldn't look at them... but she could *hear* them. The dozens of snakes protruding from the Gorgons' grimy scalps loudly hissed and licked the putrid air. Theodore clamped his hands over his ears to dampen the noise.

"Well, if you don't know which Gorgon did this to

him, how are we supposed to know which one to kill?"

"Simple," Violet replied. "We kill them all."

Theodore wasn't sure he'd heard right – in fact, he was positive he couldn't have heard what he *thought* he had. He took his hands from his ears. "I'm sorry, it's hard to make out what you're saying over the sound of a million monsters trying to eat us, but did you just say 'we kill them all'?"

Violet nodded. "That's right – every single Gorgon in the maze. It's the only way to be sure."

Theodore threw his arms in the air. "Of course! Just kill them *all*. That makes *perfect* sense." He nervously cleared his throat and continued. "But, just for the sake of argument, can I ask one more silly little question? Exactly *how* are we supposed to fight something we can't even see?"

"Simple. We fight blind."

"Ah, and there's the answer! Fight blind – how obvious. And this is something you're skilled at doing, I'm guessing?"

Violet shook her head. "Nope. Never done it before. Not sure if anyone has actually – at least, not successfully. Where do you think all these statues came from?"

"From people who totally failed the very thing you're about to try?"

"Exactly."

The shrieking of the Gorgons grew louder and Theodore could smell a nauseating odour of spoiled flesh as they closed in.

"Girl meat…" the beasts hissed. "And *boy* meat. Tenderrrr…"

Violet held her glowing axe in front of her like a blind man with a cane. "So here's what I'm thinking – their only real attack is the 'turning you to stone thing'."

"Yes. Not a bad attack, by the way…"

"True, but as long as we keep our eyes closed, it can't affect us. Without that, they basically just move really slowly, so whenever I hear one near me, I'm just going to kick off and swing at the sound."

"I see. And you feel pretty sure you're going to be able to actually hit the thing that *made* the sound?"

Violet nodded. "Definitely. I mean, my axe was created to kill monsters, right? It *wants* to taste Gorgon flesh – so I'm just going to keep swinging and give it what it wants."

"Gotcha. Sounds like a plan. Only one thing…"

"Yeah?"

"When you swing, don't swing at me."

Violet grinned. "Deal."

A familiar feeling of calm washed over her as the

Gorgons descended on them. In her mind's eye, Violet imagined every brilliant blue flash of her axe blade as it sliced through snake and gristle. In fact, she was surprised to discover that fighting blind actually seemed to *increase* her talent. It forced her to rely on her other senses – touch and balance and smell. The Gorgons nearest her shrieked in pain as she lopped off their heads, while the ones behind them continued to advance in wave after monstrous wave – but it didn't matter.

She killed them just the same.

Director Drake ran a hand over the smooth stone of Charlie Benjamin's head. It was cool to the touch. "Finally, after all this time, the boy is mine."

"What about my son?" General Dagget asked. "He's lost in the Gorgon Maze."

"Because he was foolish. You cannot protect him for ever, William – eventually, the boy has to stand or fall on his own. We all do."

"Maybe… but I'm taking a squad in there. He'll die if I don't. The Gorgons will kill him."

"Unless…" Director Drake paused, thinking. "Unless the girl kills all the Gorgons first."

"One child against the entire maze? Impossible."

"No," Drake countered. *"Unlikely.* But if she succeeds…" He turned and looked at the statue of Charlie – bone-white and shiny – then ran a manicured fingernail across the Sword of Sacrifice, now turned to stone as well. "Bring me a sledgehammer."

"A… what?" William was genuinely confused.

"If the girl kills all the Gorgons, she'll kill the one that turned the boy to stone, which will free him. If that happens, he'll escape. I cannot permit that. It has taken too long to bring him to justice."

William's eyes widened as he realised what the Director planned to do. "You can't mean to *destroy* the boy…"

"You think he prefers being a lawn ornament?" Drake shook his head. "Do as I command, William. Bring me a sledgehammer. I'll dispose of the child myself."

The General stood firm. "That wasn't part of the deal. I said I would help you capture him, even Reduce him – but I won't allow you to outright execute him. We're not murderers, Reginald."

"We are whatever we need to be to protect the common good." Drake's grey eyes were as cold as a winter wind. "Now do as I ask or I will find myself a *new* General. Bring me a sledgehammer!"

While Violet fought, Theodore struggled to keep from slipping on the floor of the Gorgon Maze – it had become black and slick with monster blood. He steadied himself against the marble statue of a short man holding an oversized mace and stifled a yawn. "Let me know if there's anything I can do. I know you've basically got this all under control, but I'm right here… just listening to you kill things… getting bored."

Violet, concentrating fiercely, didn't reply. With one mighty sweep of her axe, she chopped off the head of the nearest Gorgon. Suddenly, the statue Theodore was leaning on sprang to life.

"Great steaming piles of dragon dung!" the newly revived man roared, pushing Theodore away. "Unhand me, boy! Never sneak up on a warrior like that!"

Theodore, startled, opened his eyes for just a second and caught a quick glimpse of the man. He was short and round, with a body like a barrel. A thick, red beard covered his puffy face, which was pierced by two blue eyes. He wore a dirty grey nightgown and held a large studded mace in his right hand.

"Uh, you better close your eyes," Theodore said, quickly closing his own. "See, we're in the Gorgon Maze and, if you look at them, they'll turn you to stone again."

The man laughed. "Outrageous! Why, I've never heard

of anything quite so prepos—" He glanced at a Gorgon and was turned to stone.

"Oh, man. I think the guy's a statue again," Theodore said, blindly touching the rough rock of the man's head. "I wonder how long he's been in here."

Violet, not replying, continued swinging her axe at the monsters, chopping off the head of the last Gorgon the man had looked at. Once again, he sprang back to life.

"—terous!" the man shouted. "Gorgons? Absolutely ridiculous! Do you know who you are speaking to, boy? I am Sir Thomas Wainwright in the service of His Majesty, King Henry the Eighth, and, when addressing me, I demand that you show me the common courtesy of opening your blasted eyes!"

"Yeah, but that's what I'm trying to tell you. If you look at these monsters, they'll turn you to stone."

"Ah! Now I understand… such as the mythical Medusa?"

"Exactly!" Suddenly, Theodore felt a spray of spittle from Sir Thomas's mouth.

"Preposterous!" the man shouted. "That is a fairy story told to sprouts like you for the purpose of scaring them into obedience! No grown man would ever believe in the existence of—"

Another Gorgon slithered into view and Sir Thomas, once again, was turned to stone.

Theodore sighed. "Man, is he pig-headed. That's the second time in the last minute he's been turned to stone because he *just won't listen!*"

"Reminds me of someone I know…" Violet grumbled as she severed the head of another monster – the very one that had transformed Sir Thomas.

"—Gorgons!" the knight shouted, springing back to life. "Only a fool would believe in them and I am no fool, lad!"

"Well, if you don't believe in Gorgons, what do you think she's out here killing?" Theodore blindly kicked at the pile of dead Gorgons.

"Monsters, to be sure!" Sir Thomas replied. "And snake-headed ones at that. But to believe that they have the capacity to turn you to stone just upon gazing at them is, well – preposterous! I mean, if that were true, would I not turn to stone *right now*?"

To prove his point, he looked directly at an incoming Gorgon and was instantly turned to stone.

"I've pretty much had it with this dork," Theodore said. "Can you just hold off on killing that last Gorgon so he can stay a statue for a while?"

"Sorry," Violet replied. "To save Charlie, I've got to kill

them all." She chopped the head off the Gorgon that had most recently transformed Sir Thomas. Once again, he sprang back to life.

"You see, fool! I remain as fleshy and pink-cheeked as I've always been!" He tapped Violet on the shoulder. "Now stand aside, little girl, and let a knight of England show you how monster slaying is done!" With a ferocious shout, he raised his mace above his head, swivelled to face the nearest Gorgon... and was instantly turned to stone.

"What a fool," said Theodore.

A man with a nametag that identified him as 'B. N. Counter – Facilitator' rushed into the Reduction Room and handed Director Drake a sledgehammer. "Thank you, Mr Counter," Drake said smoothly. "I truly wish *all* my Gifted employees demonstrated the common sense and loyalty that you Facilitators do."

"You really plan to go through with this?" William asked, looking down into the Reduction Room. The hallway around him was crowded with Nethermancers and Banishers all pushing to get an unobstructed view through the shattered glass of the viewing window.

"I do," Drake replied. "Because I *must*." He turned to

the statue of Charlie. "Mr Benjamin, it is my decree as Director of the Nightmare Division that you be permanently terminated for your numerous crimes against the people of Earth, including, but not limited to, the portalling of Barakkas, the portalling of Slagguron and the killing of the Guardian, who once protected us all."

With trembling arms, Director Drake raised the heavy sledgehammer above the fragile marble statue that Charlie Benjamin had become.

"Stop this!" William said, pushing through the crowd. "This wasn't part of our agreement! This is murder and I won't allow it to happen!"

Several men in the crowd grabbed William and began to drag him away.

"What are you doing?" William yelled, fighting back. "Let me go!"

More people piled on and soon they dragged the General down the hallway and out of sight. After all, the Director was only doing what *had* to be done, wasn't he? Yes, it was extreme, but extreme times called for extreme measures, didn't they?

"Ladies and gentlemen," Director Drake said, still holding the sledgehammer aloft. "Justice is served." He swung at Charlie.

Just before the sledgehammer made contact, a portal opened in the floor directly beneath Drake and – with a startled shout – he fell into the Nether.

There was a collective gasp as the assembled Nethermancers and Banishers looked around to see who would do such a terrible thing. Finally, their eyes rested on someone who had been all but forgotten in the insane events of the last hour.

Brooke Brighton, still horribly transformed by her sacrifice, stood in the midst of the mob with purple fire crackling across her body. With a wave of her hand, she closed the portal that she had just opened.

"Where did you put him?" a Banisher demanded.

"Somewhere – *crooooak!* – safe. You're lucky too, because if I had any sense at all, I would have dropped that fiend into the 5th Ring."

"Grab her!" someone else shouted. "This is treason!"

The crowd began to advance on Brooke, yelling angrily, when a familiar voice suddenly cut through the din.

"Leave her alone."

It was Charlie Benjamin.

CHAPTER FIFTEEN
ESCAPE FROM THE SHREDDER-SHARKS

With one final swipe of Violet's axe, the last of the Gorgons in the Gorgon Maze fell dead. The snakes protruding from its scalp rattled and then went still as it dropped on top of a heap of slain monsters. It was only then, in the perfect silence of the maze, that Violet realised how loud the hissing of the snakes had been when the Gorgons were alive. She opened her eyes and was astonished by the incredible mound of them that lay in front of her, corpses cooling.

"Wow. Not bad," she said, impressed with her own handiwork.

Suddenly, Sir Thomas Wainwright sprang back to life, the hard marble of his skin turning soft and pliable once again.

"Victory!" he roared, still gripping his mace. "Turn

you to stone, do they? Preposterous! I'm as soft-skinned as the day I was born!" He looked over at Violet. "And I believe you vanquished two of the foul beasties as well, young lady. Good show! A welcome respite from playing with your dollies, I expect!"

"Yeah, right," Violet replied. "Dollies."

"Can I open my eyes now?" Theodore asked, hands on his hips. "I feel like they're going to get stuck like this if I don't do it soon."

Violet nodded. "Go ahead. All the Gorgons are dead."

Theodore blinked his eyes open. It took them a couple of seconds to adjust to the intense coloured light of the crystal walls.

"Have a look, lad!" Sir Thomas bellowed, kicking at the mound of dead Gorgons in front of him. "Quite a feat, eh? I slayed so many of the hideous monstrosities, I lost track."

Theodore laughed. "Then you must be really stupid because you slayed exactly 'none'. *El Numero Nada*. The big fat zero."

Sir Thomas's brow darkened. "And how would you know? You had your eyes closed through the entire battle like some kind of ridiculous girlie-child!"

"Yeah, and you were a statue the whole time. Violet did all the fighting, you medieval glory-hogger."

"Outrageous! I should whip you for your impudence!"

"Oh, knock it off," Violet said to Sir Thomas. "Besides, it's hard to take you seriously when you're wearing a dress."

"A dress? Young miss, this is a nightshirt and it is quite suitable for sleeping, I'll have you know! Besides, there was no time to change – I awoke to discover a large opening of fiery purple flame in my quarters and, being a noble defender of His Majesty, I immediately grabbed my trusty mace and walked through to investigate. A moment later, *you* showed up."

"A *moment* later?" Theodore repeated with a laugh. "More like five hundred *years* later."

"Preposterous! Child, you are silly in the head."

Violet sighed. "Look, Sir Thomas, here's what happened. You had a nightmare and you mistakenly opened a portal to the Gorgon Maze in the Nether – which is where we are right now – and then you got turned to stone by a Gorgon and you've been stuck here for five centuries."

"Exactly!" Theodore added. "So deal with it!"

"You impudent Gryphon turd!"

Sir Thomas ran after Theodore, who easily dodged the slower man by playing hide-and-seek around the heaped, steaming pile of Gorgon heads. He darted around a corner, nearly slamming into a woman and a man walking towards him.

"Whoa, slow down," the woman said. She wore the outfit of a Banisher from the Nightmare Division, but it seemed horribly out of date. "It appears that everyone in the maze has come back to life. Are you the one that killed all the Gorgons?"

Theodore shook his head. "Nope, not me – although if I had a weapon of some kind, I definitely *could* have. I'm good that way."

"*I* am the monster slayer you seek," Sir Thomas roared, wheezing desperately as he trotted up to the boy, his face a bright, unhealthy red. "Hold him, please. I want to hit him in the head."

"Oh, knock it off before you have a heart attack," Theodore replied. "And I already told you – you didn't kill the Gorgons, *Violet* did." He pointed to his friend, who was wiping her axe blade clean on the side of one of the dead beasts.

"Do you mean to claim," the woman said, "that the young girl over there killed every single monster in the maze? If true, that's quite something."

"Yes, she is," Theodore replied with grin.

Suddenly, a screech echoed through the crystal corridors, followed by a horrible cackle. "Murderers!" a voice shouted. "Assassins! Violators! Who dared to kill my beautiful Gorgons?"

Violet knew instantly who the voice belonged to. "The Hag Queen. You'd all better portal out before she gets here."

The woman nodded. "Excellent idea." She turned to the man beside her. "Open one up, Henry. Quickly."

Henry extended his right hand and opened a small portal back to Earth. As he and the woman leaped through, Theodore wondered how long they had been trapped in the maze. Present-day Earth might seem as strange to them as the Nether — it surely would be for Sir Thomas.

The woman turned back to Violet. "Aren't you three coming?"

Violet shook her head. "Thanks, but we have business with the Hag Queen."

"You're crazy," Henry said, laughing. "She's a boss of the Nether! If you stay, she'll kill you surely."

"Nonsense!" Sir Thomas roared. "I will slay her utterly! She will soon taste the steel of my war mace!"

Theodore rolled his eyes. "Look, seriously. We really don't need you here – you or your big mace. So why don't you just take off?"

"Nay! If there is blood to be spilt, I will spill it!"

And that was when the Hag Queen swooped down

next to Theodore on her strong, leathery wings. "You again! I invited you to come and stay with me, child – not to kill all my lovely Gorgons…"

"Ha!" Sir Thomas shouted. "It was not the boy! *I* killed them, witch – just as I will now kill you!"

Theodore groaned. "Oh, will you please shut up? I told you twenty times – you had *nothing* to do with killing the Gorgons!"

"So then it *was* you, child," the Hag cackled. "This time, memories are not the only thing I will take from you…"

"Last chance," Henry said from the other side of the portal. "Come on – jump through. You'll be safe here."

Violet waved them off. "Go on. We'll be fine."

"Suit yourself."

Henry closed the portal, locking the rest of them in the Gorgon Maze with the Hag Queen. Violet turned to her. "I'm sorry about your Gorgons, but I have something very important to talk to you about. It's about my friend Theodore."

The monster glared back and there was no kindness or pity in her eyes. "I really don't care," she said, and then attacked.

Charlie Benjamin leaped out of the Reduction Room and into the hallway beyond as the crowd of Banishers and Nethermancers closed in on Brooke.

"Stay away from her," he said, brandishing the Sword of Sacrifice in front of him.

"Or what?" replied a Nethermancer with bright red hair – Charlie vaguely remembered that the Headmaster had once referred to him as Coogan. "You'll take a swing at us with your shiny new sword?"

"If I have to."

He stepped in front of Brooke, shielding her from the approaching crowd.

"Be careful," Coogan sneered. "If you touch her, you might catch what she's got and I don't think green is your colour." Everyone laughed.

"Why are you doing this?" Charlie asked, truly mystified. "There are monsters and Golems out there – horrible things – tearing our world apart. And look at you – instead of protecting people, you're in here, trying to hurt us. We're not the enemy."

"Could've fooled me," a gruff Banisher said, his bald head shining slickly with sweat. "You got us into this miserable situation, Benjamin – you and your friends. And before justice could be dispensed, the frog – I mean the *girl* – dumped the Director into the Nether to save your sorry hide."

Charlie turned to Brooke. "You did that for me?"

She shrugged. "Someone had to. He was about to hit you with a sledgehammer. Since you were still a statue at the time, it seemed, well – unsporting."

"It was *necessary*," the bald Banisher said, "to make sure you couldn't do anything else to put this Division – and this world – in further danger. Now you can either come with us the easy way… or the hard."

Charlie sighed dramatically. "Why does everyone always give us that choice? Hey, Brooke – have we *ever* taken the easy way?"

She shook her head. "Nope. We've pretty much always been 'hard way' types."

They shared a smile then – warm and genuine – and, for just a moment, Brooke completely forgot what had happened to her, what she looked like now.

"Oh, my God, Brooke, is that *you*?" a voice cried out.

She turned to see Geoff at the rear of the crowd, dressed in his clean, new Facilitator's uniform. The handsome boy's eyes went wide with astonishment and he laughed shrilly.

"Ugh – it *is* you! You're disgusting! I told you not to go off with your bozo friends and now just *look* at you!" He jokingly elbowed a Banisher beside him. "Can you believe I actually kissed that thing?" Then he stuck his finger down his throat and made a gagging sound.

Charlie glanced at Brooke. "You want to handle this?"

"Love to."

Purple fire crackled across her and, moments later, she snapped open a large portal into the ocean of the 4th Ring. Cold, fetid water rushed through in a geyser, blasting the crowd backwards.

Yes! Charlie thought as he and Brooke were swept away along with the others. *A wetwash! Way to go!*

The raging water raced through the many hallways of the Nightmare Division, threatening to swamp the whole facility in a rising flood.

"Wow, that was some portal!" Charlie shouted as they careened past door after door like passengers on a lunatic flume ride. "All the way to the 4th Ring!"

Brooke nodded. "Yeah! For some reason, Nethermancy has got a whole lot easier since... well, since I started looking like this." She gestured to her misshapen face.

"Maybe that's because you stopped worrying about looking pretty all the time and started thinking about what's important."

"You mean like blasting Geoff in the face with freezing ocean water?"

Charlie nodded gleefully. "Did you see his expression? Priceless!"

"Well, he had it coming – they *all* did."

And that was when they saw the fin.

It sliced towards them through the water with astonishing speed. As it neared, the creature it belonged to lifted its black head above the surface, revealing row after row of razor-sharp teeth. Its eyes were silvery slits that reflected everything around them like mirrors.

"It's a Shredder-Shark!" Brooke shouted. "I must have opened the portal near a school of them!"

"A *school*? Wait a minute – you mean they come in packs?"

Brooke nodded. "If there's one in here – there's probably twenty."

Those silvery eyes widened as the creature approached and Charlie could see himself reflected in them, grotesquely stretched and wavy, as if he'd looked into a trick mirror. Suddenly, the Shredder-Shark's lower jaw unhinged and dropped further than Charlie had imagined possible, creating a deadly maw ringed with those terrible teeth. It began to scoop up everything in its path.

"Swim!" Charlie shouted. "As fast as you can and don't look back!"

But it was too late.

The Shredder-Shark was on top of them and those

razor teeth seemed to fill the world. As the raging water carried Charlie and Brooke into the large, circular hub of the Nightmare Division, he raised his sword and chopped off the monster's snout. It began to bleed profusely into the dark ocean water.

"Uh-oh," Brooke said.

"What? Did you see my sword strike? It was awesome!"

"There's blood in the water!"

"So?"

"So haven't you ever heard of a 'feeding frenzy'?"

And that was when several huge Shredder-Sharks raced into the massive hub of the Division and attacked the Shark that Charlie had wounded. The ocean around them churned violently as the massive beasts flipped and lunged while devouring their crippled prey.

"What are we going to do?" Brooke screamed as one of the giant beasts crashed down next to her, its silvery eyes glinting menacingly, white teeth flashing.

"Close the first portal and open another!" Charlie shouted back as he speared a Shredder-Shark through the head with his glowing sword. "Do it now!"

"OK! Where to?"

"I don't know! To Theodore and Violet, wherever they are!"

As Charlie swung his sword, lopping off the tail of another Shredder-Shark, Brooke closed her first portal. The blast of ocean water stopped flowing as if turned off by a tap. Then, with another wave of her hand, she opened up a new portal…

…into the Gorgon Maze.

CHAPTER SIXTEEN
THE RETURN OF A BEAUTIFUL LADY

As Violet fought the Hag Queen, she soon realised one very important thing – they weren't going to make it.

The Hag's talons were as long and sharp as swords – it was like squaring off against ten enemies instead of one – and the wind from her flapping wings made it hard to even stand, much less fight. With a sinking feeling, Violet realised that her prowess against the Gorgons had left her disastrously overconfident against this most cunning boss of the Nether.

"Out of the way, girl!" Sir Thomas shouted. "I can't swing my weapon with you standing between me and the beastie!"

Theodore stared at the man in disbelief. "Would you stop whining and start fighting? Or just hand over your stupid mace and let *me* take a whack at her!"

Theodore reached for Sir Thomas's weapon.

"Unhand the mace, boy!" Sir Thomas roared. "Never touch the weapon of a knight of England, unless ye desire to lose an arm in the process! Many is the time that I wielded this glorious instrument against a mighty foe who—"

Brooke's portal snapped open.

As the Hag Queen dived down at Violet with her razor claws outstretched, a jet of water blasted through the newly opened portal, knocking the monster backwards in a violent tumble of wings and teeth. An instant later, Charlie, Brooke and a giant Shredder-Shark rocketed through the gateway and into the maze.

"Close it, Brooke!" Charlie shouted, struggling to his feet. "Close the portal!"

Brooke did so with a quick wave of her hand, shutting off the flow of water. The giant Shredder-Shark flipped and snapped on the slick maze floor, gasping for air, knocking aside Gorgon heads like footballs.

Sir Thomas stared at the monster in amazement. "Great steaming piles of partridge poo! It's a Land Shark!"

"A what?" Theodore shouted. "It's not a Land Shark, you moron! It's some kind of shark from the Nether that just happens to be *on* land!"

"It's a – *crooooak!* – Shredder-Shark," Brooke said. "And there's an interesting story behind how it got here."

"You think?" Violet snapped, leaping to avoid the monster's teeth as it slid towards her like a runaway truck. "Can we swap stories about it *after* we kill it?"

"Stand aside," Sir Thomas yelled, raising his mace, "and I will slay the abomination for you! It will soon know the steel sting of my weapon! I will send it back to the shadows from whence it came, to the dark recesses of the night-time of its birth, to the—"

As Sir Thomas jabbered on, Charlie turned to Theodore. "Who *is* this guy?"

Theodore shrugged. "His name is Sir Thomas and he won't shut up. He's been talking about that stupid mace for ages and I have yet to see him use it."

"Uh, guys!" Violet yelled from down the hallway. "Little help with the giant shark, please!"

Charlie ran towards her and, with one nimble leap, landed on the creature's back and drove his sword into its brain, silencing it for ever.

"Thanks," Violet said with a smile.

"And thanks for killing the Gorgons and saving my life – I'm guessing that was you and not Sir Talks-A-Lot."

"Good guess."

With a cackle, the Hag Queen flapped her wings,

spraying everyone with droplets of water as she rose a few metres in the air. "Well, if it isn't my old friend, Charlie Benjamin. I should have known that this would involve you eventually. Wherever you go, boy, trouble follows."

"It's nice to see you again, Miss," Charlie replied with a deep bow.

"*Miss!* How delightful! Miss, he calls me..."

"But I will *not* miss!" Sir Thomas roared, walking towards her. "My mace is *incapable* of missing!"

"Go away, strange man," the Hag said. "And take your silly mace with you."

"This silly mace will crush you utterly, you unclean creature of filth!"

"Don't you dare talk to her like that!" Charlie said. "I won't stand for it."

"What did you say to me, boy? Do you dare to defend this impure thing?"

"How can you call something so beautiful a 'thing'? I mean, just look at her – she's gorgeous."

The Hag cackled girlishly. "Oh, *please* – attractive maybe, but gorgeous...?"

"I just say what I see. Never before have I been so mesmerised by beauty."

"What's he doing?" Theodore whispered to Violet.

She frowned. "Not sure…"

Sir Thomas walked up to Charlie, dumbstruck. "Do you have a fever, lad? Are you mentally unsound? 'Mesmerised by beauty?' The only thing beautiful about this beast will be the manner of her death, which I will soon deliver!"

"Quiet!" Charlie commanded. "I will not have you insult this lady."

"Lady!" the Hag screeched and Charlie thought it was possible that she may have actually blushed. "I'm a lady now, am I?"

"The fairest of them all…"

"Preposterous!" Sir Thomas was so red with fury that it looked like his head was about to pop off. "She is a repulsive, repugnant *witch* fit only to be spat upon and then hit in the head with a mace!"

"I warned you," Charlie said, then opened up a portal beneath Sir Thomas and dropped him through to Earth. The knight only fell a few metres before landing on the sand in front of the Nightmare Academy – but he screamed as if he had fallen a mile. With a quick flip of the hand, Charlie closed the portal, then turned back to the Hag. "I'm so sorry he troubled you, dear lady. His words were unconscionable."

The Hag screeched with laughter. "Oh, go on, you charmer! You don't mean any of it…"

"On the contrary – where others see a monster, I see a vision of loveliness."

The Hag's wide, bloodshot eyes fluttered in surprise. "Really?"

Charlie could tell that she was actually starting to believe his flattery. He nodded. "Of course… Beauty is in the eye of the beholder, and I am currently beholding a beauty brighter than even the brightest star."

"That's pushing it a little," Theodore grumbled. Violet stomped on his toe.

The Hag Queen fluttered towards Charlie on her mighty wings. She pulled stringy hair from her face, dislodging several beetles and worms. "As beautiful as I am – and as charming and kind as I am known to be – there is still the question of the girl who killed all my precious Gorgons. I know she is your friend, but she will have to pay dearly for her infamy. Don't you agree?"

"I would if she did it to harm you. But instead, she did it to celebrate you."

"She *what*?"

"Yeah, she what?" Theodore echoed.

Charlie whispered to the Hag: "The Gorgons have

been talking. They claim that their beauty surpasses even yours. But surely you know that – you, of course, know *everything* that happens in the Nether."

"Indeed, I do," she replied – although it was clear from the tone in her voice that this was news to her.

"Which is *why*," Charlie continued, "I asked Violet to get rid of the boastful beasts – there is only one great beauty in this mansion and that great beauty is *you*."

The Hag sighed happily. "Truer words have never been spoken." Reluctantly, she turned to Violet. "I suppose I owe you thanks, girl."

"Don't mention it," Violet said. "Trust me – it was my pleasure."

"As I'm sure you *also* know," Charlie continued, "there has been whispering from your Ladies-in-Hating. They envy your loveliness and there is word that they plan to kill you so that you are no longer the most gorgeous thing in the Nether."

The Hag Queen was clearly shocked by the revelation. "Jealousy! Sheer jealousy!"

"Can you blame them? I mean, just *look* at yourself."

"Without vomiting," Theodore added. This time Brooke stomped on his foot.

"Yes," the Hag Queen said, eyeing her reflection in the crystal wall of the maze. "It's not really their fault, is it? It must be so difficult to see me all the time and feel so *hideous* in comparison. I really should have more compassion for the homely creatures."

"You are as wise as you are kind," Charlie said. "However, my friends and I will gladly destroy every one of your ladies, if you wish. We certainly don't want you to be troubled by them, even for a moment."

"How wonderful you are, offering to slaughter them for little old me! You make a delicate flower like myself want to weep with happiness."

"So shall we get rid of them for you? As you know, the Sword of Sacrifice is mine now." Charlie held up the brightly glowing sword. "It wouldn't be any bother."

The Hag Queen quickly drew back, eyeing the Ancient Weapon with fear. "I… I wouldn't ask you to sully the blade of that wondrous artefact. Never fear – I will take care of my ladies myself. And if there's anything I can ever do for *you*, you have but to ask."

Charlie took a calming breath. *OK*, he thought. *Here we go – let's see if this works…*

"Well, since you're offering, there is one incredibly *small* thing." He gestured to Theodore. "He and I used to be friends – best friends in fact – until you removed all memories of our friendship from his brain."

"Indeed, I did! And delicious memories they were too!

Delightful! Delectable, even!"

"I can imagine. But here's the thing – he has now also lost the memories of the many times he and I spent walking under the stars, talking about your great beauty and wishing we could gaze upon it."

The Hag sighed wistfully. "That *is* a shame…"

"Many months ago, you took my friend Rex's memories… and then you gave them back."

"The cowboy!" the Hag gasped, her eyes glittering with delight. "Oh, how I miss his visits…"

Charlie nodded. "He talks about you all the time. And it would be so great if you could return Theodore's memories to him, so that we could *all* talk about you – about how you're the most beautiful creature that has ever walked or flown or crawled through this world or any other."

The Hag Queen suddenly grew cold. "You wouldn't be *teasing* me, would you, boy? Because that would be *terrible* for you."

"Look into my eyes and tell me if I'm being truthful."

She flew to him on her great wings.

Don't look away, Charlie told himself. *Hold her gaze. Look serious… maybe even a little lovestruck. You can do it. Just a moment more…*

The Hag Queen cackled. "You old charmer, you!"

She swooped down and snatched Theodore up in her strong arms, then leaned her head back, snaked out that long, terrible tongue and drove it into the boy's ear like a hammer driving a nail into a plank.

Theodore felt a rush of memories flood into his brain, memories of Charlie – his first and best friend. As quickly as it had started, it was over. The Hag Queen let him go and he dropped roughly to the ground.

"Are you OK?" Charlie asked, running over to him.

Theodore looked up, recognition in his eyes. "Charlie?"

Charlie nodded. "Hey, pal. It's me."

Theodore's sunny grin seemed to light up the entire Gorgon Maze. "Of course it's you! Let's see, we're in a miserable pit in the Nether, surrounded by dead monsters – who else would it be?"

They hugged.

"There…" the Hag said. "Just as you asked. Now would you all care to accompany me back to the manor to watch me slaughter my ladies? We can have tea after."

"We'd love to," Charlie said, "but I'm afraid we'll have to decline. Our world is dying and we have to save it."

"Yeah," Theodore added. "Plus, you're so darn ugly, I can't figure out whether to pity you or flush you."

The Hag Queen's eyes went wild with fury. "What did you say? Trickery! Hateful trickery!"

"Thanks, Theo…" Charlie said with a sigh.

Theodore beamed. "Don't mention it."

"You will pay!" the Hag screamed and then attacked.

As she flew towards them, Charlie opened a portal back to Earth – back to the beach in front of the Nightmare Academy – and he, Violet, Theodore and Brooke ran through. Moments later, the portal snapped closed behind them, silencing the Hag's shrieks of rage, leaving only the sound of breaking waves and the chirp of crickets in the cool, night-time air.

CHAPTER SEVENTEEN
CHARGING THE SWORD

"This has been some day," Charlie said as his friends gathered around him on the beach in front of the Nightmare Academy. "Let's see... so far I've been mind-controlled by a Chasm Wyrm, paralysed by a Shock Wasp and turned to stone by a Gorgon."

"Yeah, but at least you're better now," Brooke said, brushing sand from her green, warty cheek. "So is Theodore, and Violet never even got Reduced to begin with. But me, well – *crooooak!* – just look at me."

Charlie stepped towards her with a gentle smile. "I know you're going to want to punch me for saying this, but I actually kind of like you better this way."

Brooke snorted with laughter. "You're a moron, you know that? *You kind of like me better this way? Why –* you've always had a weird reptile fixation?

Your first crush was a newt?"

Charlie shook his head. "Nope. You may have lost your looks, but you got your Gift back in its place. I mean, you were doing some seriously awesome Nethermancy back there."

"Uh, Charlie," Theodore said. "Let me give you a little wake-up call here – she looks like a *frog*! Now I may be going out on a limb, but I'm guessing she doesn't consider that any kind of great trade-off."

"It's OK," Brooke said, looking away at the vast, rolling ocean. The silvery moonlight revealed several dolphins jumping playfully in the waves. "What's done is done. Let's just get on with this. You have the sword now, Charlie. Let's go and kill the Fifth and end this."

Charlie nodded. "We will – as soon as I charge it in the well at the Netherforge."

"Charge it?" Violet stared curiously at the glowing weapon. "Looks pretty powerful already."

"It is, but it needs to connect to the Core before it'll be strong enough to kill the Fifth – at least, that's what the Smith said. Now come on. Let's just get this done."

He raised his hand to open a portal back to the Netherforge when they heard a familiar voice.

"There you are!"

Everyone turned to see Sir Thomas stomping up the

beach, nightshirt soaked in ocean water, mace in hand.

"Oh, great," Theodore moaned. "The return of Sir Dork."

Huffing and puffing, the rotund knight walked up to them. "I thought the witch had destroyed you, children! I would have slain the foul beastie, but something preposterous happened and I fell through to this deserted isle!"

"Deserted?" Charlie said. "It's not deserted – there's tons of people at the Academy." He gestured to the great tree behind them. "Didn't you look?"

Sir Thomas nodded, causing the fat under his chin to ripple like ocean waves. "Aye. There are plenty of people, lad – but none that are *conscious*. It is as if they have been placed under a sleeping spell by a great and terrible wizard…"

Theodore rolled his eyes. "What is this nut talking about?"

"You dare call me a nut? *You're* the nut, nut! And I shall crack you open like one!" Sir Thomas raised his mace threateningly.

"OK, that's it," Brooke said and, with a wave of her hand, she opened a small portal beneath Sir Thomas. He fell into it with a shout. As soon as he was out of sight, she snapped it closed behind him, sealing him in the Nether.

"All right!" Theodore shouted. "Go, Brooke! Way to dump the mouthy knight!"

"Where did you put him?" Charlie asked.

"Same place I put Director Drake – somewhere safe. Now let's forget about him and figure out what's going on inside the Academy…"

Like fallen leaves in autumn, the students of the Nightmare Academy lay scattered across every deck, cabin and catwalk – even Mama Rose. Violet tried to shake her awake, but to no avail. It was almost as if she was in a coma.

"I don't know what's wrong with her," Violet sighed. "She won't wake up – none of them will."

"They have been cursed by the Fifth," a voice said from the darkness of the shadowy tree limbs above them. They all looked upwards.

"Xix?" Charlie asked tentatively.

The friendly Netherstalker dropped towards them on a thick line of spider-silk. "Yes, Charlie. It is me. The Queen of Nightmares herself came here, along with Edward Pinch. She… *touched* everyone… and they fell where they stood. I have kept careful watch on them. With every passing minute, they grow sicker…"

Xix gestured to Mama Rose with a bristly foreleg. Charlie noticed that the large woman's normally ruddy complexion was now waxy and pale.

"Something terrible has happened to them," Xix continued. "And it's getting worse. And that's not even the most awful part. Come."

Moments later, they entered the Headmaster's study. It was empty.

"What am I supposed to be looking for?" Charlie asked.

Xix scuttled over to the wine-coloured couch. "This is where the Headmaster used to be – and Rex and Tabitha were just in front of her before the Fifth took them."

"*Took* them?" Violet asked, alarmed.

Xix nodded. His five eyestalks bobbed in unison. "Whatever she did to everyone else, she did to them as well – and then she and Pinch portalled out with their bodies. Where they went to, I do not know."

Great, Charlie thought. *As if things weren't grim enough…*

With a quick wave of his hand, he opened a portal. "Xix, you stay here and keep an eye on things, please.

The rest of you come with me to the Netherforge."

The first thing they noticed was the bodies.

Slain Nethermancers and Banishers lay scattered across the place in crumpled heaps. "What happened here?" Brooke asked, aghast, checking the people nearest her for signs of life.

Charlie shook his head. "No idea. But I'm willing to bet that someone – or some*thing* – was looking for me and they got in the way. All of you just stay here and keep watch while I finish this." He turned and walked towards the centre of the Forge.

Violet drew her axe and followed.

"Violet, I told you to—"

"I'm coming with you – and if you even *try* to say no, I'm going to brain you with this." She gestured to her axe handle. Charlie knew better than to argue.

Soon they arrived at the large well. Inside, blue magma bubbled up from the Core.

"So… what are you supposed to do exactly?" Violet asked.

Charlie shrugged. "Just plunge the blade in, I think. Not totally sure. Let's just see what happens."

He stood in front of the low stone wall and held the

brightly glowing Sword of Sacrifice out over it. As feather-light as the weapon had always felt in his hands, it was now drawn down towards the magma with terrific force. Charlie aimed the blade downwards and, taking a calming breath, slowly lowered it into the bubbling blue lava. The second the weapon made contact, there was a brilliant explosion of light and the weight of the sword seemed to intensify a hundredfold. The magma sucked at it greedily, like a thirsty child slurping juice through a straw, and it took all of Charlie's strength just to hang on to it.

"What's happening?" Violet yelled.

"It's getting sucked in – and so am I!"

"Hang on! I've got you!"

She dropped her axe and grabbed Charlie around the waist. Even with her added strength, the entire blade was soon submerged and, moments later, so was the hilt. Charlie expected searing pain to slam through him the second his hands entered the blue liquid, but he was astonished to discover that it was actually quite cool – apparently, it was only deadly to creatures of the Nether.

"Theo, help!" Charlie yelled as his arms were pulled below the surface – he could still feel the sword in his hands even if he couldn't see it.

"On my way!" Theodore shouted, rushing over. He

grabbed on to Charlie and, together, he and Violet struggled to pull their friend away from the intense grip of the magma – but it was like playing tug-of-war with a giant.

"Keep pulling!" Charlie yelled. "Brooke! Get over here and help us!"

No answer.

"Brooke!" Charlie shouted again. "COME HERE! WE NEED YOUR HELP!"

Brooke didn't reply... but something else *did*.

"Well, well, well – what have we here?"

The voice was deep and powerful... but also strangely familiar. Charlie glanced over his shoulder and saw something that actually made him gasp in surprise.

It was Pinch.

Monster Pinch.

Towering above them, his red, antlike body looked almost brown in the shimmering blue light of the Netherforge. Brooke was gripped tightly in his mighty grasp. He smiled darkly.

"Charlie Benjamin – I've been looking for you."

"Well, that's typical. Look, Pinch, I'd love to chat, but we're in a bit of a situation here."

"You're about to be in an even worse one. Release

the sword – let the Nether reclaim it – and I'll let your friend live."

He gave Brooke a squeeze.

Charlie, still clinging desperately to the sword, quickly tried to think through his options. If he let go of the weapon, he would lose it for ever, along with any chance of killing the Fifth. But would that save Brooke from Pinch?

Charlie doubted it. Pinch was unpredictable even when he was normal. The chances of him honouring his word were even more remote now that he was transformed... but into *what* exactly?

If he was more monster than man, Charlie knew that he could potentially use the Sword of Sacrifice to slay Pinch before he killed Brooke. But what if Pinch was still more *man* than *monster*? Would the sword even affect him then? Its power was to destroy creatures of the Nether. Against humans, it was just a regular sword and it would barely scratch the surface of Pinch's massive, plated body.

"Choose!" Pinch commanded, squeezing harder. "And do it quickly – your friend cannot last much longer."

What, exactly, was *Pinch?* Charlie wondered. *Man or monster?*

Charlie turned to Violet and Theodore with a fierce gleam in his eyes. "On three, pull with everything you've got."

"Are you sure?" Violet asked.

Charlie nodded. "One… two… *three*!"

They yanked with all their might, pulling the sword free from the magnetic grip of the Core. Now charged, the weapon's miraculous power energised Charlie with the force of a lightning bolt. He held the blade aloft and it shone with the brilliance of the sun.

"You've chosen *poorly*," Pinch roared as Charlie reared back and flung the Sword of Sacrifice at his head.

Moving with supernatural quickness, Pinch snatched it from the air – it looked like a toothpick between his loglike fingers. As soon as he touched it, the sword exploded with an intense blue light that surrounded Pinch like a cocoon – but what emerged was no butterfly. Pinch shrieked in agony as his monster appearance was ripped off him like a cheap Halloween costume and he was violently transformed back to his boyish, human form. Unlike the other transformations, which had been slow and gradual, this one was fast and brutal and left a roadmap of pain on Pinch's face.

Brooke tumbled to the ground next to him as the boy

(*man*, Charlie reminded himself) struggled to his feet, holding the blazing blade in his small right hand.

"No!" Violet yelled. "He's got the sword!"

Pinch grinned crazily, the agony of his abrupt rebirth having driven him closer to madness. "That's right… I do! And it's mine now!"

"That's not fair!" Charlie shouted. "You didn't do anything to earn it. You didn't sacrifice!"

"Neither did you!" Pinch shot back. "Your friends sacrificed, but they can't hold the sword now, can they? Only Double-Threats are powerful enough to do that, Double-Threats like you… and *me*." Pinch whipped the sword effortlessly through the air.

"Give it back!"

Pinch shook his head. "If you want it – *try and take it*."

Charlie, unarmed, raced towards Pinch – after all the horror that he and his friends had suffered just to get the blade, there was no way that he was going to let it be taken from him. Pinch held the weapon out in front of him and ran straight at Charlie. The two of them headed towards each other like missiles on a crash course of mutual destruction. Then, just before they collided, Pinch did something completely unexpected—

He waved his hand and opened a portal.

Unable to stop their momentum, both Charlie and

Pinch sailed straight into it, leaving the enormity of the Netherforge behind them and falling through to Earth.

Right into the lair of the Fifth.

"NO!" Theodore screamed, watching his best friend drop out of sight.

From somewhere on the other side of Pinch's portal, Theodore, Violet and Brooke heard the familiar, chilling laugh of the monster that sometimes called herself the Fifth and sometimes Mother and sometimes simply Pearl – but whose real name was the Queen of Nightmares.

"Welcome, Charlie Benjamin," she said.

The portal slammed closed.

Deep in the throne room of the giant nautilus shell, Charlie struggled to his feet to see the Queen of Nightmares striding towards him on long, crimson legs, her purple cat-eyes swirling hypnotically under a flash of silver hair.

"Don't worry, child," she said. "Soon it will all be over and then you can sleep – you can sleep your life away."

Charlie glanced to his left to see three familiar faces laid out next to each other on the glistening floor of the lair, unmoving and deathly quiet. He was alarmed to see how pale and drawn the Headmaster, Rex and Tabitha looked – particularly the Headmaster. Her beautiful brown skin was now a mottled, pasty colour, like bad cheese, and she looked far too thin. In a strange way, she reminded Charlie of how the Guardian had looked after being poisoned.

They don't have much time, he thought. *If I can't help them soon, they'll die.*

He looked to his right to see Pinch standing there, holding the Sword of Sacrifice in an outstretched hand. It shone with the brightness of a supernova. The many Nethercreatures in the hallways and chambers that led to the throne room quickly backed away, afraid.

"Give me the sword, Pinch," Charlie rasped. "Don't let this happen."

Pinch shook his head. "I'm sorry, Charlie – but it's already far too late."

And then the Queen of Nightmares was on him and Charlie felt her strong arms wrap around his body like a winter shroud. He felt cold – numbingly cold – and his eyelids grew as heavy as a black hole that consumed even light itself. His lungs seized in his chest as he struggled to take one last gasp of air…

"It can't end like this," he said.

And then there was only darkness.

PART FOUR
THE QUEEN OF
NIGHTMARES

CHAPTER EIGHTEEN
THE SLUMBER

Brooke ran to the empty spot in the Netherforge where Pinch's portal had just slammed shut. "What are we going to do?" she cried. "Where did they go?"

"To the lair of the Fifth," Theodore replied grimly. "And Charlie is unarmed."

Violet picked up her axe and wiped the dirty blade clean on her trouser leg. "*He* may be, but I'm not. Theo, take us there. Now."

Theodore shook his head. "Sorry, no can do. I've never been inside. Charlie's the only one I know who can open portals to places he hasn't even seen – well, him and the Headmaster, I guess – but I *can* portal us to the entrance of the lair. I've seen that."

"Then do it."

"And what do we do when we get there?" Brooke asked.

Violet shrugged. "Simple. We fight."

We fight.

The words cut through the air like a knife.

"OK, stand back," Theodore said, raising his right hand.

Everyone did as he asked, narrowly getting out of the way of the portal he snapped open back to Earth – through it, they could see the burned-out landscape in front of the giant nautilus shell in Central Park.

"Let's go," Violet said, leaping into the open gateway, axe raised high. Brooke and Theodore followed.

Charlie awoke in the Slumber.

He lay on a bed of soft clover. Oversized honeybees buzzed lazily above him in the fragrant, jasmine-scented air. The blue sky was filled with candyfloss clouds that seemed eager to form themselves into recognisable shapes – Charlie spotted a fluffy bunny on the horizon, chased by what looked like a smiling hippopotamus.

What is this place? he wondered as he got to his feet.

He expected his joints and muscles to ache from all the abuse they had suffered, but was surprised to discover that he was remarkably pain-free. In fact, truth be told, he felt *great* – maybe never better. The air was warm and sweet and the music of songbirds filled the air. The gorgeous creatures flapped around on large, luminous wings the colour of fruit – cherry reds, bright oranges and even plum purples.

The place was absolutely delightful – but where *was* he?

Glancing around, he knew only that he was in a vast, hilly meadow full of clover and wild flowers. It seemed to go on for miles until finally ending at a treeline that marked the beginning of what looked to be a green and sunny forest. Beyond the trees were mountains – wide and grassy at the bottom, leading to smooth, rocky expanses higher up until finally giving way to snow-covered summits. In the centre of the mountain range was a pillar of white light, shimmering gloriously, reaching high into the sky like a finger pointing up to heaven.

The whole place was magnificent… and yet strangely familiar.

Charlie struggled to identify the odd feeling of *déjà vu* he was experiencing. He had been here before – he *knew* he had – and yet he was also certain that this was somewhere new.

But how could that be?

And then, like an electric shock, the answer came to him.

He was in the Nether.

Or at least some weird, alternate version of it.

The lush meadow where he stood was the 1st Ring, although in the Nether it was rocky and barren. The forest beyond was the 2nd Ring, although the trees here looked nothing like the spooky, skeletal monstrosities found in the shadow version of this world. The mountains were clearly the 3rd Ring and, beyond them, Charlie imagined he would find an ocean – the 4th Ring – but he was certain that here it would be warm and inviting – a stark contrast to the foul, chill expanse of water in that other place.

But the clincher was that wondrous spire of clean, white light that ascended into the heavens. In the Nether, it was a red and churning column that speared down through an alien sky, right into the Inner Circle.

"Charlie Benjamin!" a voice called out in a southern accent as thick as cream. "How you doin', child?" Charlie turned to see Mama Rose cheerfully waving to him from the waist-high grass. He was thrilled to see her… and yet he knew that back on Earth, she lay comatose in the Nightmare Academy, her body rapidly disintegrating, her life force draining away. "I'm so glad you're here!" she exclaimed, walking towards him with a broad smile. And then he noticed other people in the meadow – youngsters, many of them from the Academy.

What was going on?

"Mama Rose... where are we?" Charlie asked, pushing his way through the clover to reach the cheerful woman.

She shrugged. "No idea, but I *like* it. Don't you?" She breathed in deeply and smiled as soon as the fragrant air hit her lungs. "Wow! It sure is marvellous here. In fact, I don't ever want to leave."

"Yeah," Charlie replied. "I know it's nice and all that, but back on Earth, you're unconscious. And your body is, well... it looks like it's *dying*."

Mama Rose glanced skyward, her expression as serene as a swan's. "Let it. I don't ever want to go back there, Charlie. I truly don't."

This place is a trap! Charlie suddenly realised. *It's beautiful on purpose – designed to lower your defences and make you so comfortable that you don't ever want to try and find a way out!*

Which opened the door to a really big question: Was *there a way out?*

"Have you seen the Headmaster?" Charlie asked.

Mama Rose nodded. "She and Rex and Tabitha were

all just here. But they... they wanted to *leave*, if you can imagine such a thing!" She laughed then – great rolling gales of laughter, as if the very notion of wanting to leave such a wonderful place was beyond comprehension.

"Where did they go?"

Mama Rose turned and pointed to the spire of white light that Charlie knew must lead to this world's version of the Inner Circle.

"The centre," she said. "They flew there on birds." As if to demonstrate how this was possible, Mama Rose whistled pleasantly and, moments later, a lemon-yellow songbird descended from the sky and landed at her feet, chirping sweetly – it was almost twice as big as she was. "See? Just like this one here."

"Yeah. I see. Thanks." Charlie walked towards the bird, which immediately lowered a wing to the ground so that he could climb up on to its back. Its feathers were soft and downy.

"Oh, Charlie, *must* you?" Mama Rose gently scolded. "Why can't you just stay here and relax, like the rest of us..." She gestured to the other students from the Academy. They were running happily through the meadow. "We can have *such fun* together!"

Charlie smiled. "I know... but I have to go. I have to

try and help us. Take care, Mama Rose…"

With that, the songbird flapped its wings and rose high into the air with Charlie securely tucked away on its back. He hadn't communicated what he wanted to do – he'd only *thought* it – but the creature seemed to understand just the same. It banked, cutting a path through the warm air, and then headed straight towards the beam of light in the very centre of this odd and dangerously inviting place.

The buildings around Central Park were in ruins.

Golems had ravaged most of the structures, reducing them to heaps of concrete and steel. The sky was filled with a thick, choking smoke.

"They've destroyed the city!" Theodore yelled, looking around in dismay. He and the others stood at the edge of the park, some distance from the entrance to the massive nautilus shell. "The place is decimated."

"And *empty*," Brooke added. "I haven't seen a single person."

Violet nodded. "Me neither. They've all run off – or been portalled out by Nethermancers from the Division. The city is in the hands of the monsters now."

The thought seemed to incense Theodore. "Man! I

can't believe everyone just took off running. Whatever happened to staying and fighting?"

"How?" Brooke replied. "We've seen what these – *crooooak!* – Golems can do. Heck, the military attacked them and it was like the soldiers weren't even there!"

"Well, if there's no way to fight them, then what are we going to do about these two?" Violet gestured to two giant Fire and Water Golems that were stationed on either side of the shell's entrance to protect it from invaders. "I mean, if we can't get past them, then this is all over before it even begins."

Brooke seemed baffled. "When *what* is all over? I'm still not even clear what the plan is."

"The *plan*," Violet said, "is to fight our way into the lair, find Charlie and help him. But first we've got to figure out how we're going to get past these two Golems."

"Let *me* take care of that," Theodore said with a chuckle. "It's easy peasy mac and cheesy – trust me."

Then, to Brooke's astonishment, he ran straight at the massive creatures.

"What's he doing?" Brooke gasped, turning to Violet.

"No idea…"

Theodore raced towards the monsters as fast as

his spindly legs could carry him. "Hey! Look at me, you big goons! Down here!" The gargantuan beasts swivelled their heads in Theodore's direction. "That's right, you overgrown matchstick and you big bottle of water! I'm Theodore Dagget! Come and get me, you morons!"

They did.

Moving with surprising swiftness, the Water Golem surfed straight at Theodore on a wave of its own creation while the Fire Golem leaped towards him, leaving behind molten slag with every footstep.

"I can't watch," Brooke said, shutting her eyes tightly.

At the last possible second, Theodore swerved to the left and ran straight between the legs of the Fire Golem. The Water Golem corrected its course, chasing him.

"No!" Violet shouted, suddenly realising what Theodore's plan was.

The Water and Fire Golems collided, creating a massive explosion of steam that destroyed both beasts instantly.

"Theodore!" Violet screamed, knowing that her friend could never have survived such a cataclysm. "THEO!"

"What?" a voice said calmly from behind her. Violet spun round to see Theodore stepping out of a portal. He smiled. "Don't get so hysterical. Just before they hit each other, I summoned a portal and escaped into the Nether. I'm not *stupid*. Geez."

Violet stared at Theodore, then punched him in the arm so hard that he dropped to the ground. "Don't you… EVER… scare me like that again!"

"Uh, OK," Theodore replied, massaging what he knew was going to be a massive bruise. "As long as you don't ever *punch* me like that again."

"OK, what's next?" Brooke asked, walking up to the newly unprotected entrance to the lair. "What do we do now?"

"Now we go inside," Violet replied, "and kill everything that gets in our way." Saying that, the young Banisher strode into the lair of the Queen of Nightmares.

Hang in there, Charlie, she thought. *The cavalry is on its way.*

CHAPTER NINETEEN
THE LAIR OF
THE FIFTH

In the heart of the giant nautilus shell, the Queen of Nightmares gently stroked Charlie Benjamin's cheek. He lay on the floor, comatose. Already his skin was beginning to grow cold.

"You have done well, Edward," she said, turning to Pinch. Her purple cat-eyes fixed on the brilliantly glowing sword in his hand. "Why did you bring that wretched thing with you?"

Pinch shrugged. "I… I didn't mean to. Things were just happening so fast and, before I knew it, it was in my hand and then we were *here*."

"Well, open a portal and get rid of it. Throw it into the well at the Netherforge. It makes me… uncomfortable."

Pinch held her gaze a moment then looked away. "I understand why you feel that way, but…"

"But *what*?"

Pinch raised the blade and cast his eyes lovingly along its razor-sharp edge. "It's just so beautiful and, when it's in my hands, I feel so *powerful*."

The Queen of Nightmares suddenly lowered her head and growled. The sound was so deep and frightening – so *unlike* her – that Pinch actually stumbled backwards.

"Powerful?" she hissed. "Don't be a fool, Edward! You have drunk from me twice and, once you cast away that revolting sword, I will allow you to drink from me a third time – a *final* time – and then your monstrous form will return and become permanent. *That* is true power. It comes from who you are – not from some ridiculous trinket, like the one you now hold."

Pinch swallowed nervously. "If it's so ridiculous... why are you afraid of it?"

She shot him a ferocious look that said, more clearly than words, that killing him would be a pure pleasure – if such a thing were possible while he still held the sword. "Get rid of it," she said finally. "Right now. Right this *second*."

Pinch considered. "No. I think... I think I'll wait a bit."

The jewel-like eyes of the Queen of Nightmares drew down to angry slits. "In that case, Edward – we are going to have a problem."

As Charlie flew through the Slumber on the back of the lemon-yellow songbird, he marvelled at how like – and utterly *un*like – this place was from the Nether. The layout was the same, but the specifics were all different.

He crested the snow-capped mountains of the 3rd Ring – from this height, they looked like scoops of vanilla ice cream. And then he was swooping down and skimming over the ocean of the 4th Ring, which was as clear and as blue as the one in the Nether had been murky and grey. Sea animals leaped and dived cheerfully in the waves, seeming to follow him, chasing after each other in some kind of friendly game.

Moments later, he left the ocean behind and then sailed out over the crystals of the 5th Ring. Unlike the horrible mustard colour of the ones in the Nether, these were clear as diamonds and they all seemed to point in the same direction – towards the glorious column of light that surrounded the Inner Circle. It sparkled and shimmered enticingly, beckoning Charlie forward.

Soon he was through it and soaring over the Inner Circle itself. Back in the Nether, the four palaces of the Named were dark and gothic, each one perfectly reflecting the evil of its owner – but here they were as light as the homes of the gods on Mount Olympus, with crystalline domes and pillars of gleaming white marble.

But that wasn't even the most surprising thing.

High in the sky, in the very centre of the statuary-filled courtyard that all the palaces shared, a pearly platform seemed to float in the air – although, as Charlie neared it, he realised that it was actually held aloft by arching bridges that led to it from each of the four castles.

Hovering in the middle of the platform was an enormous shadowy being, towering and translucent.

There was something familiar about it…

It took Charlie a moment to recognise what it was, before he suddenly realised that it was actually *the Fifth* – the Queen of Nightmares herself – or at least the version that she chose to present here in the Slumber. The very existence of the shadow creature seemed impossible given the brightness of the sun – and yet there she was, framed by a shimmering oval of light directly behind her. At her feet were three small dots. Even from this far away, Charlie knew who they were: Rex, Tabitha and the Headmaster.

He imagined the songbird drifting down to drop him off next to them and, to his amazement, that's exactly what it did. It swooped through the air and then came to a smooth stop on the platform, quickly lowering a wing to allow Charlie to get down and join his friends.

They seemed unsurprised to see him.

"Mr Benjamin," the Headmaster said with a sleepy smile. "I assumed you would join us sooner or later."

"How long have you been here?" Charlie asked. "And how do we get out?"

"We don't, kid," Rex replied lazily. "Heck, when we first got here, we thought the same as you – that there *had* to be a way out. But, you know what? After you spend a little time here in the Slumber, you realise that there ain't a way out and, even if there *was*, why would you ever want to leave? It's so… peaceable here."

Charlie turned to Tabitha. "You don't feel this way too, do you?"

The Nethermancer grinned and stretched out on the platform, moaning pleasantly. "Why wouldn't I? It's nice here, Charlie. You'll see. You just have to give it some time. It *grows* on you."

It grows on you.

More like feeds *on you*, Charlie thought darkly. *On your willpower, on your desire to escape it and, finally, on your life…*

"Why fight it, Mr Benjamin?" the Headmaster said, her brightly coloured dress fluttering in the sweet breeze. "I've tried and… it's no use. No use at all."

"But, back on Earth—"

"Back on Earth, my body is a crippled husk," she interrupted. "Here I'm in no pain, I'm never hungry and nothing is ever expected of me." She sighed contentedly. "Here I can be... happy."

Charlie shook his head. "Not for much longer. Your body is dying. Pretty soon it will be dead and so will you."

The Headmaster shrugged. "So be it."

So be it.

It horrified Charlie to realise that the Headmaster was lost to him – to everyone really, including herself. She was the strongest of them all, but her time in the Slumber had broken her, just like the Chasm Wyrm in the Nether had broken *him*, if only briefly. The Slumber was like a deep and pleasantly warm ocean that lulled you out, away from shore, and by the time you realised you'd swum past the point of no return, it was too late.

You drowned with a smile on your face.

"Charlie Benjamin..."

Charlie turned to see the dazzling shadow image of the Queen of Nightmares looking down at him. She was grinning.

"Listen to your teachers. They are wise. They care for you."

Charlie shook his head. "They've been too long in this

horrible place. You've corrupted their minds. But not mine. I'm getting out."

"There is no way out."

"That's a lie. The only way to keep people from trying to escape is to make them *not want to*. That's the reason you made it so nice in here – because if people wanted to leave, they might eventually figure out *how*."

"You are smart, Charlie Benjamin. But that will not help you. No one has ever escaped the Slumber. Join your friends. Enjoy the time you have with them before you die."

Charlie walked defiantly towards her. "I could say the same thing to you. Edward Pinch has the Sword of Sacrifice. How long before he slays you with it?"

For just the briefest of moments, Charlie saw a look of fear flash across her face.

"Edward Pinch has already disposed of the sword," she said. "He has thrown it into the well of the Netherforge. It has returned to the Core."

"That's a lie."

Again there was that brief flash of fear, and Charlie knew he was getting to her.

"You dare to question me?" the shadow form of the Queen of Nightmares thundered.

"I know Pinch. And I know that he wants power more

than anything else. The sword gives him that."

"So do I. When he drinks from me, he becomes transformed."

Charlie shrugged. "See, and that's exactly the problem – what you give to him, you can also take *away* from him. But no one can take the sword away."

"You could," she replied mockingly. "If you were out of the Slumber."

Charlie smiled slyly. "So you admit he still has it."

Fury erupted over the shadowy face of the Queen of Nightmares. Then, like an ocean wave erasing footprints on the sand, her look of rage was replaced by an unreadable expression of calm – but Charlie knew that, underneath, there lurked a terrible anger.

He had wounded her.

"Play as many games as you like, Charlie Benjamin. You will perish playing them – but not before I have drained your life force to fuel my destruction of your world."

"I'll find the way out. Trust me."

"There is no escape! The Slumber is sealed tight! Your portals do not work here!"

Charlie knew that much was true. He was in the Slumber in mind only – not in body – so there was no way to physically escape through any portal he knew of.

Unless… unless there was some *other* kind of portal.

He looked past the shadowy presence of the Queen of Nightmares to the radiant oval just behind her. It looked so familiar. In fact, he thought it looked just like —

A portal.

"Step aside," Charlie said.

"And why would I do that?"

"Because I think that's a portal behind you – a portal back to my body – and I'm going to step through it and then I'm going to kill you."

The Queen of Nightmares laughed, but Charlie detected a note of hysteria. "Go ahead and try, Charlie Benjamin."

Summoning his courage, Charlie walked forward. "You know what I think? I think you have no way to protect that portal. This isn't really you – it's just the shadow version of you."

"We are connected. We affect one another. My strength is her strength, and hers is mine."

"I think you're powerless. You're like the Wizard in *The Wizard of Oz* – all bark and no bite – telling everyone to 'ignore the man behind the curtain'. You're not the Fifth, you're just her shadow, and to walk right through you and into that portal, all a person needs is the simple belief that they *can*."

Charlie stepped right up to her.

Suddenly, the Queen of Nightmares roared and swiped at him with a massive, shadowy hand. The open palm hit him with the force of a truck and knocked him backwards on to one of the bridges that led to the platform.

"It doesn't require belief, boy!" she shrieked. "It requires fighting!"

Charlie staggered to his feet.

"OK then… let's fight."

Violet, Theodore and Brooke battled their way through the Queen of Nightmares' lair. The shimmering, organic hallways – which had been so carefully crafted by the Shellweavers – were now black and slick with monster blood.

Violet's axe flashed against the incoming tide of creatures as Theodore and Brooke summoned portals underneath the ones that approached from behind. The two Nethermancers were like gunslingers in a shoot-out – fast, accurate and very deadly.

"Above you!" Theodore shouted, glancing over his shoulder to see a flock of Netherbats swooping towards

Violet. But before the Banisher even had a *chance* to respond, Brooke opened a portal in front of them and the bats sailed harmlessly through it and into the Nether.

"Dang, Brooke!" Theodore exclaimed as he opened a portal around a leaping Dangeroo. He quickly snapped it closed, slicing the monster in half. "You're like a portal-making machine now!"

She laughed. "I may look like a frog, but my portals are as pretty as a princess."

"You got *that* right!"

They advanced steadily, slaying every creature that swarmed their way – Netherstalkers, Hags, even Darklings. Soon they were within sight of the throne room.

"Almost there," Violet said, covered in black ichor, chest heaving. "Charlie should be close..."

Inside the throne room, the Queen of Nightmares heard Charlie's friends approach. "They are stubborn creatures," she growled. "Like you, Edward."

"What would you have me do, my lady?"

"Destroy the sword."

"And if I refuse?"

"Then destroy *them*."

Pinch found her answer curious. "Why don't you just touch them and put them into the Slumber? The more humans you have there, the stronger you will become."

"I could, but I won't – because I want to see them die. Or, to be more exact, because I want to see *you* kill them."

"After all I've done for you, you're still not sure where my loyalties lie?"

She shook her head. "If you were truly loyal, you would rid yourself of that hideous weapon."

"This weapon is the only thing keeping me alive! Without it, eventually I'll do something you don't approve of – like Barakkas, Slagguron and Tyrannus – and then you will destroy me."

She dismissed his concern with a wave of her hand. "I can't do to you what I did to them. I created them to begin with, you see – which allowed me to *un*create them. With you… I have no such power."

The fight outside the throne room drew closer… and it didn't sound like the creatures of the Nether were winning. The cackling of Hags was abruptly turned into a spurting gurgle; the song of the Silvertongues was silenced by the snicker of an axe blade.

"Destroy the sword before they arrive," the Queen of Nightmares hissed, "and I will let you drink from me. You cannot be transformed while you hold it. You cannot be made *magnificent*." She leaned down to whisper in Pinch's ear. The Sword of Sacrifice vibrated angrily in his hand, centimetres from her vulnerable body, desperate to taste her alien flesh. "We are family now, Edward. Here we stand, at the moment of our greatest triumph. Open a portal to the Netherforge and drop the sword into the Core. Let me *transform* you. I will let you drink until you have had your fill. I will give you enough blood to become… astonishing."

Astonishing.

That sounded good, but Pinch was wracked with indecision. Even though the world of humans had rejected him, he knew that if he wanted to wield the sword, he would have to *return* to that world and pray that it embraced him. On the other hand, the world of monsters had welcomed him and it would take only one more sip of the blood of the Fifth to be transformed *permanently*. The choice was not a moral one – Pinch had left morality behind long ago – he was now only concerned with being on the winning side, whatever the cost.

"Rid yourself of the weapon," the Queen of Nightmares purred, "and join me for ever. Become my most special baby."

"Don't do it, Pinch," another voice said and Pinch

looked up to see Theodore enter the throne room. "She lies – you know she does. Take the sword and kill her with it."

The Queen of Nightmares glared at Theodore. "Do not listen to him. Destroy the sword and then destroy them. *All* of them."

"You can't trust her, Pinch," Brooke said, stepping up behind Theodore. "This doesn't have to end badly. You can be a hero today. Kill her now."

"I… I don't know," Pinch replied, trembling.

The Queen of Nightmares spoke then, her voice kind and soothing. "When their world despised you, I took you in. I welcomed you as one of my own. I made you my son."

My son. That sounded nice.

"Kill her!" Violet yelled. "Kill her now! You're the only one of us that can wield the sword and do it!"

"Join me, son," the Queen of Nightmares said, her voice as loud and clear as a church bell. "Join me and rule the world of humans by my side. Seek your vengeance against them! Claim your power! BECOME THE MONSTROUS THING YOU WERE BORN TO BE!"

"You're right," Pinch said with sudden finality, turning to her. "You took me in when they did not. I'm sorry to have ever doubted you. I'll love and protect you forever… Mother."

And, with that, Pinch roared in fury and ran towards Violet and the others, the Sword of Sacrifice held high above his head, shining brightly.

Violet reacted instantly. She rushed towards Pinch, axe raised. Her weapon was clearly no match for his and her Banishing skills were nowhere near the equal of a Double-Threat's – but thoughts of doubt did not cloud her mind. She was a weapon of destruction, as Theodore liked to say, and had only one goal in mind.

Stop Pinch.

As the two of them neared each other, time seemed to slow. Violet knew she was only going to get one shot at this before Pinch took her out. As he brought the Sword of Sacrifice down towards her, she leaped into the air and leaned back, almost parallel to the ground, her legs pointing straight at her wild-eyed opponent like a spear.

Then they made contact. Violet's feet slammed into Pinch's ribcage so hard that she heard bones crack. Pinch flew backwards from the enormous force of the blow, missing her with the blade by less than a hair's breadth. He tumbled helplessly across the throne room, end over end, sword flashing crazily, then began to arc back down… straight towards the Queen of Nightmares.

"No!" she screamed as Pinch, still gripping the Sword of Sacrifice, slammed into her, mistakenly *hacking off her upper left arm.*

It fell to the floor with a wet thump, spasming and jerking. Pinch landed next to it, the force of the impact knocking the weapon from his hand. The blade slid across the glossy floor before finally coming to rest in the very centre of the chamber.

"What have you done?" the Queen of Nightmares shrieked, staring in shock at her missing arm as Pinch crawled away, horrified. "WHAT HAVE YOU DONE TO ME, YOU FIEND?"

Back in the Slumber, Charlie raced towards the colossal shadow version of the Queen of Nightmares. He was in terrible pain from her last attack and already he could feel the supernatural force of the Slumber greedily sapping away his will to fight. But he knew that his only chance was to keep coming after her and hope that he found a weakness. As he neared her, she pulled back two of her massive hands, preparing to strike him once again… and then suddenly she collapsed to the ground, eyes wild with pain and confusion.

"What's wrong?" she gasped as her upper left arm disappeared. "What's happening to me?"

Something bad, Charlie thought gleefully as he ran towards her. *Bad for you, good for me...*

Then he leaped up over her prone body and sailed, headlong, into the enormous, silvery portal beyond.

Charlie sat up in the throne room of the nautilus shell to find it in utter chaos. The Queen of Nightmares was clutching at the protruding bone of her missing arm, shrieking furiously, while Pinch wailed in sorrow.

"I'm so sorry, my lady! It was an accident! I never meant to do such a thing!"

"Then fix it!" she screeched. "Get rid of the miserable sword before it causes more harm!"

The sword.

Charlie saw it in the middle of the vast throne room, shining brilliantly. He leaped to his feet and ran towards it.

"Charlie!" Violet shouted. "You're back!"

Pinch, seeing Charlie, scrambled after the weapon as well.

No… Charlie thought. *Don't let him get it!*

But the traitorous man was much closer to the blade than Charlie. With a cackle, Pinch dived for it—

—*and promptly disappeared into a portal that had snapped open right in front of him.*

"Bye bye, Pinch," Brooke said, slamming closed the portal she had just opened. She turned to Charlie. "You can thank me later – now get that sword!"

Charlie did. His fist closed around the beautiful black hilt of the weapon and instantly, he felt its energy flow through him like a raging river. Holding the blade aloft, Charlie turned towards the Queen of Nightmares, fire in his eyes.

"This ends now."

"You think so? Let's find out!"

She raised her three remaining arms. With quick flicks of each hand, she summoned Fire, Air and Earth Golems inside the cavernous throne room.

"Destroy him, my babies!"

They swivelled their brutish heads towards Charlie.

"Charlie, watch out!" Brooke yelled and began to run towards him, but Violet yanked her back.

"Let him handle this – it's his fight now."

"But we can't just sit here and do *nothing*!"

Just then, a portal popped open in the throne room

and Pinch leaped through it, returning from the Nether.

Violet smiled grimly. "Who said we're going to do *nothing*?"

As Charlie waded into his fight against the Golems, Violet, Brooke and Theodore closed in on Pinch. Even though it was three against one, Pinch was a Double-Threat, which made victory against him by no means certain.

"Get out of my way!" Charlie shouted, swinging the Sword of Sacrifice at the Air Golem. Instead of passing through the massive creature, as soon as the blade made contact, the Golem disintegrated with a howl – its death cry sounded like the high-pitched shriek of a hurricane.

Wow! Charlie thought. *This sword is pretty awesome!*

He spun around and swung at the advancing Earth Golem. It collapsed against the might of the blade like a sandcastle falling to an incoming wave. Then, with a sideways leap, Charlie turned to the Fire Golem and brought his weapon crashing down. As soon as it connected, the Fire Golem exploded in a blast of embers that reminded Charlie of cinders swirling up a fireplace.

"Don't get too pleased with yourself," the Queen of Nightmares hissed. "You've only just begun to fight!"

Her long, crimson hands began to flick rapidly – an orchestral composer conducting a symphony of death –

and Golem after Golem sprang to life in the throne room, thundering towards Charlie. He swung at them with increasing confidence, destroying every single one with just the briefest touch of the blade, as he advanced steadily towards the Queen.

"Edward!" she screamed. "Get rid of him!"

"Of course, my lady!" Pinch yelled back, as he fended off Violet's attacks while dodging the many portals that Theodore and Brooke threw beneath him. He glanced over his shoulder to see Charlie slay the last of the new Elemental Golems that the Fifth had summoned.

"EDWARD!" she shrieked. "HE'S HERE! HELP ME!"

Purple fire exploded across Pinch as he summoned a portal directly underneath Charlie. Leaping to avoid it, Charlie flung himself forward – but he didn't clear the portal completely. He tumbled into it and, grasping wildly, managed to snag the nearest leg of the Queen's massive throne, stopping his fall.

"Charlie!" Violet yelled. "Hang on!"

The Sword of Sacrifice grew heavy in Charlie's hand. He looked down to discover that he was hanging above the magma well in the Netherforge. Even from this distance, it sucked at the Ancient Weapon with violent force.

"Close the portal, Edward!" the Queen of Nightmares screeched. "Cut off the boy's arm! Do it now! End this!"

Pinch began to snap the portal closed – when Theodore punched him so hard in the face that he collapsed to the ground.

"That portal doesn't close till *I* say it does!" Theodore yelled, then leaped on to Pinch's chest and began to pound him.

Charlie, meanwhile, struggled to hold on to the sword – but it was a losing battle. The Nether Core sucked at it with an almost human desperation and the Ancient Weapon slipped lower and lower in Charlie's sweaty hand until he was only clinging to it with the tips of his fingers. The Queen of Nightmares walked to the edge of the portal and stared down at him, a triumphant smile on her face.

"You've lost, Charlie Benjamin. It looks like the Sword of Sacrifice will now claim at least *one more* sacrifice."

And then Charlie lost his grip on the wondrous weapon.

The sword that they had all fought so hard to obtain fell down through the chill air before finally crashing into the well of bubbling blue magma that led to the Core of the Nether.

It bobbed there momentarily… and then was gone.

"No…" Charlie gasped. "It can't be…"

"Oh, but it is," the Queen of Nightmares replied, her purple, jewel-eyes glittering with hate. She leaned down and caressed his trembling hand – the one that still clung desperately to her throne. "Now it's time to send you back to the Slumber."

"Sure," Charlie replied. "Right after I send *you* to the Core…"

He reached up with his one free hand and grabbed the Queen of Nightmares by her silvery hair. Letting go of the throne, he yanked her with him through Pinch's portal and into the Nether, where they both fell, tumbling end over end, towards the well of the Netherforge far below.

CHAPTER TWENTY
THE CORE OF THE MATTER

Charlie and the Fifth hit the magma with the force of a meteorite, sending great sheets of the bubbling blue liquid high into the air. The Queen of Nightmares wailed in agony as it boiled her alive.

"IT HURTS! IT KILLS!!!"

She scrambled to escape, but Charlie clung to her tightly and they were both quickly pulled under by the irresistible draw of the Nether Core. Even though the lava didn't hurt Charlie, he couldn't breathe and his lungs desperately ached for air. The Queen of Nightmares thrashed wildly in his grip and he could see chunks of her alien flesh ripping away as they plunged deeper and deeper into the well.

So this is how it ends, Charlie thought. *I'm going to drown here… but at least I'll take her with me.*

Down they hurtled as Charlie's lungs screamed for oxygen. The Queen of Nightmares spasmed in his arms while the magma tore at her – but soon her struggles became less violent.

Will it kill her? Charlie wondered. *At least before it kills me?*

He doubted it. He could feel himself ready to pass out from lack of air, which he knew would give her an opportunity to swim back up through the lava and possibly escape.

And then his arm touched something—

The Sword of Sacrifice.

He reached out and grabbed it. The blade energised him instantly and – with his last remaining breath – he let go of the Queen and then plunged the magnificent weapon straight into her terrible black heart. As soon as he did so, she exploded in a geyser of green blood, putrid flesh and wicked dreams; the only thing that escaped was her final shriek of agony, which bubbled up through the magma and into the endless night of the Nether.

The Fire Golems descending on the Royal Swedish Opera in Stockholm suddenly exploded into clouds of cinders and were blown away. In Prague, the Water Golems hurling themselves out of the Vltava River were vaporised, leaving behind only mist, which soon dissipated. The German capital of Berlin, under siege from a horde of thundering Earth Golems, abruptly fell silent when the monsters crumbled like ancient ruins, falling to the ground in great heaps of sand. And Air Golems – viciously dismantling the Eiffel Tower in Paris – vanished like wisps of smoke in the strong wind that swept across from the River Seine.

And the Golems weren't the only thing destroyed along with the Queen of Nightmares.

Her terrible creation known as the Slumber also vanished the very second her dark heart stopped beating. Back at the Nightmare Academy, Mama Rose awoke and glanced around to discover that all the students were regaining consciousness, finally free of the grip of that awful place.

"Well, *that* was interesting," she declared, rising to her feet.

Far away, deep in the throne room of the evil one's lair, the Headmaster opened her eyes and looked over to see Rex and Tabitha beginning to stir as they escaped the seductive hold of the Slumber and rejoined her in the land of the living.

"Headmaster!" Brooke shouted. "Are you OK?"

The Headmaster nodded weakly. "The Fifth is dead?"

"We think so," Violet replied. "Charlie must have killed her."

"Dang, I knew that kid would come in handy," Rex said with a grin, propping himself up on his elbows. "Where is he?"

Violet and Theodore glanced at each other uncertainly.

"Gone," Theodore said finally, his voice cracking with emotion.

"Gone?" Tabitha asked, struggling to her feet. "What does that mean?"

Violet shook her head. "It means we don't know. He fell into the Netherforge. We haven't seen him since…"

There was silence as everyone struggled to process that – and then the quiet was broken by the unwelcome sound of Nethercreatures stirring in the hive of hallways and chambers beyond the throne room.

"They'll be coming for us," the Headmaster said. "The Fifth may be dead – and her Golems along with her – but the rest of the monsters in our world are still alive and on the attack. We must leave."

"But what about Charlie?" Theodore asked as the sound of the Nethercreatures drew closer.

The Headmaster closed her eyes tightly. "He has always been a resourceful boy. We must hope that he has one last trick up his sleeve…"

"He better have," Theodore said, looking behind him. Pinch stood there beside the empty throne of the Queen of Nightmares. "Because if anything happens to him, I'm going to take it out on *you* – you traitor!"

Pinch shrugged. "Everyone dies sooner or later. For Charlie, it's just sooner – that's all."

"You filthy little—"

Suddenly, a portal snapped open in the air above the throne room and Charlie Benjamin came crashing through, along with a flood of magma from the well in the Netherforge. He slammed into the floor of the lair on all fours, gasping for breath.

"Charlie!" Violet yelled.

"Yeah. It's me."

He staggered to his feet and, still holding the Sword of Sacrifice, stepped out of the jet of bubbling blue liquid that poured into the room. Theodore, overcome with emotion, grabbed his best friend and gave him a big hug.

"You idiot! I thought you were GFG!"

"Gone For Good?" Charlie asked.

Theodore nodded. "Don't you ever scare me like that again!"

It was a joyous reunion – for the few seconds it lasted. Within moments, dozens of Nethercreatures swarmed into the throne room. Charlie raised his sword – ready to defend them in spite of his exhaustion – when he realised that, for once, he didn't *need* to. The magma from the

Nether Core, which still poured in from the open portal, spilled across the floor of the throne room, instantly incinerating every monster it touched.

Netherstalkers wailed as their spindly legs came into contact with the deadly stuff. Darklings – low on the ground to begin with – were quickly overcome, as were the Dangeroos leaping into the chamber. Their muscular legs shot out from under them as soon as they landed and, within moments, they were consumed by the wave of lethal lava. As it spread across the floor, Pinch glanced down to see that its outermost edge was nearly touching the severed arm of the Queen of Nightmares. He leaped towards it and snatched the limb out of harm's way before the magma could destroy it.

"What are you doing?" Charlie asked, aghast.

Pinch smiled. "Becoming *glorious* again! One final sip from the blood of the Queen is all I need to permanently return me to my beautiful, monstrous form!" He raised his hand and opened a portal to the Nether. "Till we meet again…"

"You're not going anywhere with that!" Theodore shouted and leaped towards him. The treacherous man stumbled backwards, and Theodore was only able to grab on to the hand of the severed arm.

"Let it go!" Pinch shouted.

"Make me!"

They began tugging at the strange prize like two kids fighting over a wishbone at Christmas dinner. Suddenly, three of the Queen's long fingers – gripped securely by Theodore – snapped off from the rest of the hand. He stared down at them in revulsion.

"Eww."

"Enjoy!" Pinch said with a cackle, then turned and leaped into the Nether, still holding the arm of the horrific creature that Charlie had just killed. Moments later, the portal slammed closed behind him. Pinch was gone.

Magma began to overflow the vast chamber, flooding into the rest of the lair, leaving slain Nethercreatures in its wake.

"We'd better go," Brooke said and, with a wave of her hand, she opened up a portal of her own. Within moments, everyone had escaped through it, leaving the inside of the vast nautilus shell as still and quiet as a tomb.

At first, Charlie thought he had returned to the Slumber, and he could tell from the look on the Headmaster's face that she thought so too.

But then he realised where they really were – in the grassy meadow that led to the banks of the lake where the Trout of Truth lived. It was the only place in the Nether that was both beautiful and monster-free. Charlie breathed in deeply, finally allowing himself to relax a little.

"I can't believe it's finally over."

"Thanks to you, Mr Benjamin," the Headmaster said.

Charlie shook his head. "Thanks to *all* of us. I never could have got the sword to begin with – heck, I never could even have survived long enough to use it – without my friends."

"I stand corrected. You have all been… spectacular."

The youngsters beamed.

"There you are!"

Everyone turned to see Sir Thomas, still in his nightshirt, gripping his mace like a hammer. The deranged knight had made his way across the white stepping stones that led to the large, flat rock in the very centre of the lake where the Trout of Truth lived. Dark, glassy water surrounded him on all sides.

"Once again, you magicked me, you nasty children!"

"Who's this clown?" Rex asked, hitching his thumbs in his belt loops.

Theodore sighed. "Ah, just this dumb knight we picked up." He cupped his hands around his mouth and shouted, "Hey, Sir Thomas, you might want to get away from there and come back to shore!"

"Preposterous!" the knight yelled back. "I will go where I please, sprout! I have examined much of this unnatural area and now I intend to explore this lake!"

The children glanced at each other, grinning.

"This is going to be *funny*," Theodore said.

Charlie walked towards the water. "Seriously, I'd listen to Theodore if I were you, Sir Thomas! Get off the lake before you say another word!"

"Do you dare to threaten a knight of England, lad? I have been slaying men and beasties since before you were born!"

"*Way* before," Theodore muttered.

"My trusty mace and I are a fearless team! We have killed many vicious enemies in our world and slaughtered countless Gorgons in your own – no thanks to you! I am the bravest man alive!"

Theodore chuckled. "And here it comes…"

Sir Thomas stood defiantly on the white rock at the very centre of the lake as Theodore started counting.

"One… two…" As soon as the boy said 'three', a gigantic, glistening fish – the Trout of Truth – exploded from the depths and, to Sir Thomas's astonishment, swallowed him whole. The great Trout slammed back into the water with a mighty crash.

"I take it he's *not* the bravest man alive?" the Headmaster asked with a sly smile, and everyone burst into laughter. They all waited patiently for the Trout of Truth to resurface and spit out Sir Thomas… but the great creature was nowhere to be seen. "My goodness. Sir Thomas must have been *quite* a liar for the Trout to keep him under this long…"

Just then, the Trout of Truth burst out of the water and hurled Sir Thomas from its mouth. The knight, covered in fish goop, flew through the air before slamming ungracefully into the ground. He struggled to his feet, and then slipped back down on the patch of Trout slime beneath him.

"Preposterous!" he roared. A fresh round of laughter erupted from the group.

"What's he doing here anyway?" Violet asked, smiling happily – it struck Charlie that it had been a long time since he had seen her do that.

"This is where I put him," Brooke replied. "It's the only place in the Nether I know of that's safe. That's why I dumped Director Drake here too."

At the mention of the Director, the laughter died away.

"Drake's here?" Tabitha asked. "I haven't seen him…"

Rex shook his head. "Me neither, but I doubt that

snake is eager to let us find him. Heck, I bet he's probably hiding out there in those trees somewhere." The cowboy gestured to the woods at the far side of the lake. "One thing's for sure – if you put him here, he's *still* here unless he got help gettin' out."

Charlie glanced at the sheer mountain walls that surrounded them on all sides. Rex was right – they kept the monsters of the Nether out... but they would also have kept Director Drake *in*.

"Go and find your father," the Headmaster said, turning to Theodore. "And bring him here immediately. In fact, bring *everyone* here." She turned and looked out over the glassy lake where the Trout of Truth lived. Her eyes grew distant and cold.

"It is time to settle the matter of Director Drake once and for all."

CHAPTER TWENTY-ONE

DRAKE

Purple portals snapped open across the meadow in front of the lake. To Charlie, the brilliant circles of light looked like a swarm of fireflies. Banishers, Nethermancers and Facilitators from the Nightmare Division strode through on to the soft grass, led by William Dagget, their General. His son, Theodore, walked beside him.

"We're back!" Theodore shouted as he approached Charlie and the rest of the group. "Everyone was pretty easy to find. After the Golems died, they all headed back to the Division."

"To celebrate your victory!" William said with a smile. The crowd that formed behind him began to cheer.

"Charlie! Charlie! Charlie!"

William walked up to him and – to Charlie's

astonishment – actually shook his hand. "Excellent work, son. *All* of you. What you accomplished today is nothing short of amazing."

"No thanks to you and the Director," the Headmaster said pointedly.

"I accept that. I made choices that I thought were in the best interests of my son, and I was wrong."

"Heck, don't let yourself off so *easy*!" Rex said, walking up to the man and clapping him on the shoulder – but not in a friendly way. "Let's be honest. It wasn't just your son you were thinkin' about – you also made choices you thought were in *your own* best interests. In fact, the only time you showed any decency at all was when Drake-the-snake actually tried to *kill* Charlie. The kids told us all about it."

William nodded. "I agree. My behaviour has been... shameful." He turned to the crowd behind him. "Which is why I hereby announce that I'm stepping down as General of the Nightmare Division."

There were a few gasps of surprise – but not as many as Charlie had imagined there might be. William gestured to Charlie and his friends.

"The seven people that stand here before us were placed in exile unfairly. They received our scorn, our fear and our hatred – but they did not deserve it. I take my share of the blame. All of you believed they were guilty of conspiracy and of the murder of the Guardian because I – along with Director Drake – *said* they were." He frowned. "And yet… you are not entirely blameless."

The people shifted uncomfortably, but William didn't flinch.

"You knew that what we were doing to them was wrong – knew it in your gut, just as I did – and yet you didn't protest. Only these seven had the courage to stand up and fight for what was right." He turned to Charlie. "I apologise to you, from all of us – me especially."

He began to applaud them then. Soon the rest of the crowd followed. Charlie and his friends were overwhelmed by the wave of adulation.

"You deserve this," Violet said to Charlie.

"We *all* do," he replied, putting his arm around her.

"There you are!" a voice suddenly cried out. Everyone turned to see Director Drake bolting from the cover of the treeline. "I've been waiting *for ever* for someone to come and rescue me since these vicious traitors arrived! William – take them into custody immediately!"

William didn't move.

Drake, truly angry now, stormed up to him. "What don't you understand about the word 'immediately'? Are you *still* being defiant? I said, apprehend them!"

"It's over, Reginald."

"Over? What are you *talking* about?" Drake nervously licked his thin lips.

"Charlie Benjamin is not a traitor. We accused him of killing the Guardian in the lair of the Named, but he wasn't the one who did it… *you did*."

"Lies! Vicious lies!" Drake screamed and then, before anyone could stop him, he pulled William's sword from its sheath and stabbed it into his former General's side.

"Dad!" Theodore shouted, rushing to his father, who collapsed to the ground. He pulled the sword from the wounded man's body. "No… this can't be happening. You'll be OK…"

William looked up at his son and smiled weakly. "So will you." He touched Theodore's cheek with one rough, calloused hand. "I'm so proud of you, son."

"No… Dad…" Theodore, tears spilling down his face, turned to Drake in a rage. "I'm going to kill you."

Drake stumbled backwards, pushing frantically through the crowd. "Stop him, all of you! The boy means to murder me – he just said so! He comes from a family of traitors and cowards! *I am your Director!*"

But no one tried to stop Theodore. Still holding his father's sword, now stained with blood, he pursued the Director with a blind fury. The sword was heavy in his hand – he was not a Banisher after all – but he didn't seem to notice. Vengeance was the only thing on his mind.

Drake, seeing the wrath in the boy's eyes, turned and ran in the only direction left open to him – out on to the lake, across the stepping stones.

"I had to do it, boy," he shrieked, leaping gingerly from rock to rock. "Your father was a liar! And liars must be punished!" Finally, the Director arrived at the flat, white stone in the very centre. The water around him was deep and still. "I told you, I did not kill the Guardian – Charlie Benjamin did! Charlie Benjamin is evil! He must be destroyed! I have nothing but your best interests at heart! All of you! You must believe me – *I'm telling you the truth!*"

And, with that, the Trout of Truth leaped from the dark lake and swallowed Director Drake whole. It crashed back down in a massive explosion of water. Soon it was gone from view.

Theodore stood on the shoreline as waves from the enormous creature lapped over his feet. The lake rocked and rippled violently and then, eventually, grew still. Everyone waited breathlessly for the Trout to reappear and spit Director Drake back out.

And they waited. *And waited*.

And, finally, after many minutes of waiting, Charlie

spoke. "I don't think the Trout is going to let him go."

Theodore whistled in amazement. "Do you seriously mean Drake's just going to stay in there *for ever*? I mean… can he actually *survive* in there?"

No one ventured an answer – no one knew really – and the Trout of Truth never surfaced. After centuries of protecting its precious lake from the terrible poison of lies, the most ancient and honourable creature in the Nether had finally found a person so full of them that it imprisoned the foul man in the slimy depths of its cold, dark stomach, perhaps never again to see the light of day.

"He's going to be fine," the nurse in the Nightmare Division's hospital wing said to Theodore some hours later as he sat with his friends at his father's bedside. "His wound is serious, but it's not life-threatening."

Theodore exhaled in relief. "Thank you." He glanced down at his dad. William was fast asleep – the sedatives had kicked in over an hour ago.

"We should let him rest and go to the ceremony," Violet said, gently rubbing Theodore's back. "They're going to be officially giving the Headmaster the job of Director."

"Yeah, we don't want to miss that," Charlie added cheerfully. "I can't think of anyone who deserves it more."

Theodore nodded. "Definitely." He looked down at his father again. "He's a good guy, right? I mean, *ultimately*?"

"Yeah," Brooke said with a smile. "Just like you. *Ultimately*."

They all laughed then and things seemed a little better.

The High Council chamber of the Nightmare Division was packed and the Headmaster was already standing at the dais when Charlie and his friends entered. They quickly took their seats at the very back of the large room, careful not to make a noise and interrupt the proceedings. After patiently waiting for them to sit down, the Headmaster surveyed the crowd and began to speak.

"My friends. What an adventure we have had together. It is with great honour and deep humility that I acknowledge your offer of the position of Director of the Nightmare Division. And it is with that *same* honour and humility that I must now decline."

Everyone glanced at each other, confused.

"Why is she doing this?" Violet whispered.

Charlie shrugged. "No idea."

The Headmaster calmed the clamour with a wave of

her hand. "Although the four Named Lords of the Nether are now gone, along with the Fifth and her terrible Elemental Golems, our world is still overrun with the Monster Army that they assembled – and many more monsters are growing strong in the Nether even as we speak, just waiting to come to Earth through our nightmares.

"There are two reasons for my decision to decline your offer. The first is that, in spite of our most recent triumph, our job here at the Nightmare Division is not yet over – in fact, it has only just begun. And it will most likely go on for many years, which means that someone must train the next generation of monster hunters." She smiled. "That someone is me, as it has always been. Therefore, I choose to remain in my position as Headmaster of the Nightmare Academy.

"The second reason – perhaps the more *important* one – is that I am not the best candidate for the job." She sighed wearily. "I stand before you, weak in body and tired in mind. We have all been living, for far too long, in a dark and frightening age. The last Director led us astray and we are now lost in the wilderness. We need someone fresh and bold and full of *hope* to lead us back to the light. Someone with skill and courage and honour. Someone untainted by the old and unafraid to open the door to something marvellous and new. That person is here with us today, sitting quietly in this High Council chamber… and his name is Charlie Benjamin."

Charlie froze.

Did she really just say my name? he thought. *Seriously?*

"But he's just a *student*, you are surely thinking. How could he possibly run something as complicated as the Nightmare Division – he doesn't know any of its rules or politics!" The Headmaster grinned pleasantly. "In answer to your unspoken question – no, he does not. Which is precisely *why* we need him to lead us. It is not what's in Mr Benjamin's *head* that makes me want to follow him, it is what's in his *heart* – and I would follow his kind heart anywhere, even to the ends of this good, green Earth and beyond."

Rex stood up at the front of the chamber. "So will I."

"And me," Tabitha said, standing as well. "I will follow Charlie Benjamin."

There was silence then as all the Nethermancers, Banishers and Facilitators glanced at each other, wondering what their fellow monster hunters were going to do.

Finally, Coogan, the red-haired Nethermancer, broke the quiet and stood. "I will follow him too."

"So will I," said the bald Banisher who had screamed

for Charlie's blood after the boy had been turned to stone by a Gorgon. And then, one by one, everyone in the room began to stand.

I will follow him… I will follow him… I will follow him…

Finally, Charlie Benjamin and his friends were the only ones left sitting. Theodore rose to his feet. "Well, I pretty much *have* followed Charlie everywhere and I can promise you this – there won't ever come a day when I'll stop." He grinned. "I will follow him."

"And so will I," Violet said, standing.

"And so will I," Brooke echoed, rising as well.

"It is unanimous," the Headmaster proclaimed, beaming. "Ladies and gentlemen of the Nightmare Division, I present to you your new Director – Charles Benjamin."

The applause was deafening.

"Go on up there, *Charles*," Theodore said, smiling from ear to ear.

Charlie stood and walked towards the dais down the long centre aisle of the High Council chamber. He could vividly remember making that same walk less than a year ago, absolutely terrified, as he strode forward to face Director Drake for the first time.

Now *he* was the Director. What a difference a year made…

The Headmaster stepped aside as Charlie took centre stage. He waited for the applause to die down before he spoke.

"Well, this is… pretty unexpected. I don't know what to say really. Like the Headmaster mentioned, we have a lot of work to do. There are monsters everywhere and more are popping up in the Nether every second. I don't exactly know what the answer to that is, but I do know *this* – we have to keep on fighting."

He looked out across the sea of expectant faces, unsure how to continue. What did they want from him? What was there to say? And then his eyes locked on to Theodore, Violet and Brooke, staring up at him, smiling proudly, and the words flowed easily.

"Less than a year ago, I pretty much didn't have a friend in the world. Outside of my parents, everyone was scared of me and it sort of looked like that's how I was going to spend the rest of my life – alone and unwanted. And that's a really frightening thought, you know? Scarier than all the monsters I've ever faced, trust me." He smiled. "But then I found out that there were other people out there just like me – people like *you*. And that made everything seem a whole lot better. And even though things were getting more and more terrible, having friends gave me the strength to want to change that. And I think that's the key really. *You are not alone…* and neither am I. We'll battle the monsters together – not for ourselves, but for *each other*. Because friendship is the most important thing in the world, and the world is worth fighting for."

And with that, Charlie Benjamin stepped off the dais and walked down the aisle to rejoin his friends, his ears ringing from thunderous applause.

CHAPTER TWENTY-TWO
AN OLD FRIEND

There's my boy!" Mr Benjamin exclaimed, snatching Charlie up in his arms. He hugged him tightly. "You look fine and fit, son!"

"Stop hogging our child," Mrs Benjamin said, pulling Charlie to her. "And he does *not* look fine and fit – he looks entirely too thin, as usual."

"I guess I was referring more to the fact that he's *alive*."

Olga smiled warmly. "He certainly is at that."

Charlie threw his arms around both of them. It had been one week since he'd been named Director of the Nightmare Division and this was the first chance he'd had to be with his parents. "It's so great to see you. Did you get menaced by any monsters while I was gone?"

Barrington nodded. "Indeed, we did! And I racked up quite a few kills, thank you very much." He turned to his wife. "How many Netherstalkers did I destroy with my baseball bat? Nine?"

"Five," she replied.

"A minimum of eight," Barrington confirmed with a nod. "I'm quite sure of it."

"And I discovered that I have no tolerance for Hags," Olga said. "None at all. In fact, two of them landed on our porch and I took care of them quite handily, I think."

Barrington laughed. "That she did – although now I need to get a new three-iron. She twisted my previous club like a pretzel." He leaned towards Charlie and whispered, "Hag heads are harder than you think."

"They sure are," Charlie said, smiling. He led them across the warm sand in front of the Nightmare Academy, towards the giant tent that had been erected. A party to celebrate Charlie's appointment as Director was in full swing. Underneath the colourful, wind-whipped fabric, delicious piles of food lined long, wooden tables – fish taken wriggling from the ocean just hours earlier, juicy fruits that grew wild on the island and a variety of tropical drinks.

"Hey, it's the Three Bs!" Theodore chirped, walking up, a cheerful grin on his sunburned face. "Mr Benjamin, Mrs Benjamin and Boy Benjamin!"

Charlie smiled. "You're totally sunburned – you know that, right?"

Theodore nodded. "I lack the necessary melanin in my skin to resist the sun's crippling rays."

"Either that or you lack the necessary *sense* to get *out* of the sun's crippling rays."

"That's another sillier way to put it, but yes." Suddenly, Theodore clapped a hand over his mouth. "Oh, Charlie, I'm so sorry! I shouldn't have said it like that, given your new position. What I mean is that's another sillier way to put it… *Director*."

Charlie couldn't help but chuckle. "Much better."

"Come on, princess!" a voice thundered across the dance floor in the middle of the tent, and Charlie recognised Rex's Texan twang immediately. If Barbie and Ken dolls had different 'looks', then so did he – this was Tropical Rex, who looked pretty much like Regular Rex except that he wore shorts and sandals instead of jeans and cowboy boots. "Get over here and shake a tailfeather with the fella you can't get outta your mind."

Rex grinned at Tabitha, who stood on the opposite side of the tent, talking to a group of girls. She looked particularly pretty, with her fiery red hair set off by an emerald sundress that fluttered playfully in the breeze. She turned to him.

"What is broken in your brain that makes you think I can't 'get you outta my mind'?"

"Hey, it's not your fault. I mean, after all, who could? Just look at me!" Rex spread his arms wide as if to say 'check out the merchandise'. "Besides, I'm the *General* now, thanks to the new Director." He winked at Charlie and Charlie, smiling, waved back.

"Well, I'm busy right now," Tabitha said coyly. "So why don't you go and dance by yourself for a while, *General*?"

Rex grinned. "Sorry, no can do. See, I'm too much man to keep to myself, darlin'. I'm *concentrated*. If I don't spread me around a little, I might just explode." With that, Rex unlooped the lariat clipped to his belt and, with a quick, graceful motion, he sailed it across the tent and lassoed Tabitha around the waist.

"You've finally lost your mind, haven't you?" she said, staring at him incredulously.

"No, ma'am – it just looked like you needed a little encouragement is all."

He began to pull her towards him and her shoes left two trenches in the sand. It was such a bizarre and funny sight that even Tabitha had to laugh. "You're crazy, you know that?"

"Naw, *you're* crazy – for me."

"Really? Then why would I do this?"

Purple fire crackled across her and, moments later, she opened up a portal directly beneath Rex. He fell into the Nether with a shout. Unfortunately for Tabitha, he was still holding on to the rope around her waist and yanked her, screaming, into the Nether right after him.

Everyone burst out laughing – Charlie hardest of all. He looked over to see Mama Rose and Professor Xix chuckling along with the Headmaster. Already, she was beginning to look much healthier.

"Why don't you go on and see some of your friends, son?" Barrington said. "Your mother and I don't need babysitting."

"I might even drag your father out on to the dance floor," Olga added, "and see if those old bones of his have any new moves left in them."

"Sounds good," Charlie replied, smiling. He glanced over and saw Violet sitting on a bench by herself, her long hair loose and flowing in the warm breeze. He hadn't seen her looking this relaxed in, well, *ever*.

"What you doing?" he asked as he walked over.

She held up a sketchbook with a drawing of a dragon – it looked remarkably like the Chasm Wyrm they had fought.

"Cool!" Charlie said. "I didn't know you'd started drawing again."

Violet nodded. "It makes me happy. I can't be a Banisher all the time, you know – I've got to do some fun stuff too. I'm trying hard to remember that." She looked up at him with a serious expression. "So should you – *Director*."

"Yeah."

She set the sketchbook down. "Tell you what. I saw Theodore and Brooke walking off together just a minute ago. Want to join them?"

"Definitely."

They took off, running, and a few minutes later, found their friends sitting together by the Banishing caves.

"Want some company?" Charlie asked.

"Sure," Brooke replied. "That is, if you don't mind hanging out with a frog."

Violet smiled. "Maybe you just need to be kissed by a handsome prince. At least, that's how it works in fairy tales."

Theodore raised his hand. "I'll kiss her. Seriously. I'm not a prince exactly, and I don't know if I'm handsome enough, but—"

Brooke leaned over and kissed him on the lips. It was gentle and sweet. When she pulled away, she turned to the others. "Well? Anything?"

They stared at her, waiting for some sign of a transformation. Finally, Charlie shook his head. "Nope. Sorry, Brooke."

She smiled. "Well, it was a nice kiss anyway. Thanks for trying, Theo."

"Any time."

"Don't I get a shot at it?" Charlie asked.

Brooke nodded. "Sure. What harm can it do?"

Charlie leaned over, closed his eyes and gave her a kiss. It was just as sweet and gentle as the first time he had kissed her, here on this very same beach.

"So… anything magical happening?" Brooke asked, after Charlie leaned back. The other three shook their heads sadly.

"You know, it's really not fair," Violet said with a sigh. "Brooke is the only one whose sacrifice is permanent – or at least seems to be."

"We'll find a way to change you back, Brooke," Charlie said. *"Trust me."*

"I do, Charlie."

The four of them sat, enjoying each other's company, chatting and throwing pebbles into the crashing surf. For the first time in a long while, everything seemed good.

"So what's the plan, Stan?" Theodore asked finally

when the sun was low in the sky, painting the beach a glorious fire-orange. "How do you figure we can end this Monster War once and for all?"

Charlie shrugged. "Wish I knew. The only thing I'm sure of is we have to try something different. The more monsters we kill, the more of them spawn in the Nether, which means this war will never end. There has to be another way. Something new. Something big. Something that we haven't seen or even thought of before…"

Suddenly, Charlie's eyes grew wide. He stood up.

"What?" Violet asked.

"That's it! Something new – something we haven't seen or thought of before! I have to leave!"

"Now?" Brooke asked. "But we're in the middle of your party!"

"There's no time to waste." Charlie turned to go, then looked back at his friends one more time. "By the way, I love you guys."

"Same here," Theodore said as the rest of them replied with a nod. Charlie was amazed to see that it almost looked as if Violet and Brooke's eyes were shiny with tears.

"Well, see you soon," he said awkwardly and, with a wave of his hand, he opened a portal deep into the Nether, stepped through it and was gone.

Even though he had seen glimpses of the Inner Circle before, Charlie had never actually been there in person. The sky above him churned a fiery red, which made the twisted statuary in the massive courtyard seem to flicker and shift ominously. The four palaces of the Named that stood at each corner of the courtyard were silent – silent and still – and they loomed over everything like temple gods.

In the Slumber, which was a mirror image of the Nether, a giant platform had hovered above the courtyard in the Inner Circle, held aloft by bridges from each palace. On that platform there stood a giant portal – the one Charlie had run through to get back to his body.

Was there also a giant portal here in the Nether? he wondered. *Just like there was in the Slumber? And if there was, where would it lead?*

He looked up. A dark platform, covered in wicked-looking runes, hung high above the Inner Circle – just like the one in the Slumber. In the centre of the platform, an enormous portal hovered mysteriously. It was a deep, swirling green. Charlie couldn't see through it to the other side.

"Wow," he muttered.

"Wow indeed," a deep voice replied, startling him.

Charlie recognised that voice immediately and his heart nearly stopped beating.

"It is a pleasure to see you again, Charlie Benjamin."

Charlie slowly turned to look at the palace directly behind him. Standing there on the obsidian steps, smiling pleasantly, was Barakkas the Rager.

"How?" Charlie gasped, staring in awe at the giant, blue-skinned beast, easily ten storeys tall. "You were killed."

Barakkas shook his head. "Eons ago, the Fifth created me in the Otherworld – me and all the Named. We served her like good children but, instead of thanking us, she destroyed us. *But she did not kill us.* She sent us back to the Otherworld – there, beyond the Monster Portal." The great beast gestured to the churning green portal that hung in the air high above them.

"Your arm!" Charlie exclaimed, looking at the hand that Barakkas pointed with. "That's the same one I cut off – it's back!"

Barakkas nodded. Charlie could hear the *swish* of the Named Lord's enormous horns as they sliced through the air. "Yes. There, in the Otherworld, we were reborn, healthy and whole." He flexed his reconstituted right hand.

"So why did you come back through the Monster

Portal?" Charlie asked. "Why did you come back here to the Nether?"

Barakkas shrugged. "This is where my palace is. This is where I belong." The massive creature strode down the stairs towards Charlie. His thick hooves sparked showers of flame with every step.

Charlie backed away. "What about the others? Slagguron and Tyrannus and Verminion?"

"Slagguron and Tyrannus chose to remain in the Other." Barakkas sighed deeply, as if their choice disappointed him. "As for Verminion – he is dead. The Fifth couldn't return him to the Otherworld because he had already been killed by Edward Pinch." Barakkas smiled, showing many sharp teeth. "Speaking of Pinch, where *is* he anyway? I would so much like to talk to him…"

From the look on Barakkas's face, Charlie was pretty sure that the great beast wanted to do more than just *talk*.

Charlie shrugged. "Don't know exactly. The last time I saw him, he was going to drink the blood of the Fifth and transform himself into a monster permanently. He's on your side now."

Barakkas shook his head. "No. Pinch is on no one's side but his own."

Deep in the heart of the lair of the Fifth, the thing that used to be Edward Pinch walked alone.

"Kill them… all of them," Monster Pinch muttered, his giant ant legs crumbling the blue lava rock beneath him. "They hate me… and I hate them. Every last one. Filthy creatures. Someone needs to *lead* the monsters of the Nether. Someone needs to *destroy* the humans. Destroy the *boy*!"

Pinch laughed – although it sounded more like an insane shriek as it echoed through the many hallways and chambers of the shell.

"*I* will lead them. Yes! And someday, I will rule the *world* and they will all bow to me!"

He laughed again as he anxiously paced back and forth across the deserted throne room – a hollow, empty shell of a man in a hollow, empty shell.

The air in the Inner Circle was chill and smelled vaguely of copper. It reminded Charlie of the smell of blood.

"Do you plan on killing me?" the boy asked, hands on his hips.

The great beast shook his head. "Not today. I have… mellowed."

"Somehow I find that hard to believe."

Barakkas shrugged as if to say 'believe what you want'. Charlie turned back to the Monster Portal. It swirled and churned ominously.

"So… what's on the other side?"

"Answers," Barakkas replied. "Probably the very answers you seek. The Nether was not always this way – it was once bright and beautiful." He looked up at the red, alien sky. "It can be that way again."

Bright and beautiful.

The words reminded Charlie of the Slumber – but maybe the Slumber was just a pale reflection of what the Nether could once again become.

"How?" Charlie asked. "How can we make it like it used to be?"

"That you will have to discover on your own, Charlie Benjamin."

"Through the Monster Portal?"

The Named Lord nodded.

"Then help me," Charlie said finally. "Take me there."

The great beast thought a moment, then lowered his right hand to the ground – the very hand that Charlie had cut off many months before. Charlie took a breath and stepped on to it. Barakkas lifted the boy up and gently deposited him on the platform beneath the glowing green portal, careful to avoid touching the Sword of Sacrifice, which hung at Charlie's waist, shining brightly.

"Thank you," the boy said.

"My pleasure."

Charlie turned to the giant portal and tried to imagine what lay beyond. He couldn't.

"Well, see you when I come back – *if* I come back."

"Goodbye, Charlie Benjamin."

"Goodbye, Barakkas."

And then Charlie Benjamin – the youngest Director the Nightmare Division had ever known – drew the Sword of Sacrifice and, raising it high, stepped through the Monster Portal and was gone.

READ ON FOR
EXCLUSIVE
EXTRA CONTENT

An excerpt from:

THE NIGHTMARE DIVISION'S GUIDE TO THE NETHER: Drake Edition
A message from Director Drake

Welcome Facilitators, Banishers and Nethermancers. My edition – the Drake edition – is to be considered the only definitive version of this guide, replacing all others, and is restricted to those Rank 3 and above. If you have not yet attained Rank 3, STOP READING IMMEDIATELY and turn yourself in to the authorities for punishment. To succeed in our endeavours, RULES MUST BE FOLLOWED and CHAOS AVOIDED!

Now that we have removed the unqualified from reading this extremely confidential document, I'd like to address a few common questions. First of all, what is the purpose of the Nightmare Division? Quite simply, our mission is to protect the citizens of Earth from the monsters of the Nether. We do this in several ways:

We banish Nethercreatures back to the Netherworld.

We train people who have shown an aptitude for the "Gift" to use it wisely or not at all, thereby preventing them from portalling monsters in the first place.

We Reduce those who have an uncommonly powerful "Gift" – to stop them from mistakenly bringing the very worst of the Nethercreatures into our world (see pg. 212: "The Unfortunate Case of (*name removed*) and the Portalling of Verminion").

By utilising these techniques, we seek to control the flow of monsters to our planet. Many people ask me if I am uncomfortable heading a division filled with employees who have the "Gift" when I do not have it myself. To them I say – how ridiculous! Does a football coach need to be on the field, getting tackled by 1000 kilos of sweaty men in order to decide on the team's formation? Of course not!

The truth is that my lack of the "Gift" puts me in a perfect position to be objective. Unlike certain former Directors, I do not allow myself to be swayed from the task at hand by empathising with your difficulties. This has led some of you to accuse me of being insensitive. You claim I don't understand how hard and, often, deadly your jobs are.

To that I say – NONSENSE!

I'm sure it's very tough to do the work you do... but do you know what else is tough? LOTS OF THINGS! Touching your nose with your tongue, for instance. Don't believe me? Try it.

My point is that the world is full of challenges that we must ALL overcome. Just because many of you have to summon your deepest, darkest fears in order to do battle with the monsters of our nightmares, please do not think that you're any stronger or better than the rest of us. Do you see me crying whenever I have to put on a tuxedo to attend a champagne dinner or write an order to have someone Reduced? Of course not!

Now that we're all on the same page, I invite you to dive into this extensively researched and incredibly useful guidebook. Inside, you will find a Map of the Nether; a Beastiary of many of the Monsters of the Nether (see pg. 86 for detailed information on the greatly overrated "Trout of Truth"); a glossary to help you understand commonly used terms (i.e. "Wetwash", "Portal Barricade"); a history of our Allies in the Nether (see pgs. 147-154 for great detail about our special relationship with the "Guardian" and pgs. 182-189 to learn much about the NetherForge and its ruler, the "Smith").

And that's just the tip of the proverbial iceberg.

Keep this guidebook handy.

Keep it safe.

Keep it away from those who would do us harm.

Sincerely,

Reginald Drake
Director of the Nightmare Division

An excerpt from:

THE NIGHTMARE DIVISION'S GUIDE TO THE NETHER: Drake Edition

LORDS OF THE NETHER:
What you need to know!

The Netherworld is ruled by four horrific monsters, each of whom controls a palace in the Inner Circle (see pgs. 73-78 "Inner Circle: Why You Have No Business Being There"). Although little is known about these beasts, their names are a matter of record. They are: Verminion, Barakkas, Slagguron and Tyrannus.

The Lords of the Nether appear to have one unified goal – to escape from the Nether and come to Earth. There is evidence to suggest that they have a larger, apocalyptic plan that they intend to unleash upon our world after arrival. Little is known about this plan, but there are three indisputable facts:
Their plan involves something called "The Fifth".
It would be catastrophic to our world if it ever came to pass, therefore:
We must NEVER let it come to pass.

Please carefully read the following sections for more detail on each Lord of the Nether:

VERMINION

Often referred to as "Verminion The Deceiver", he is the most well known of the Lords of the Nether and yet we still know very little about him. Of all the Lords, he is the only one known to have escaped from the Nether (see pg. 212: "The Unfortunate Case of (*name removed*) and the Portalling of Verminion").

He has been in our world for over 20 years. Where he resides, we do not know, although it believed that he is in the process of drawing Nethercreatures to him for the purpose of assembling an army.

Description:
Like all the Lords of the Nether, Verminion is enormous. His crab-like body could easily cover a baseball diamond with enough room to spare for his gigantic claws to reach into the stands and snap many attendees in half – thankfully, this has not yet occurred.

His shell is heavily plated and is thought to be impervious even to missile attack. Although the US Military claims to have "one big son-of-a-gun of a bomb that could crack that bad boy open like a cooked lobster – bring butter", we sincerely doubt it.

Class:
Like all Named Lords, Verminion is not ranked by Class number. He is unique.

Combat Tactics:
It's all about those giant claws. Witnesses report seeing Verminion cut a city bus in half as easily as "I can snap a pretzel stick". While the "pretzel stick" analogy leaves something to be desired, the point is well taken.

In addition to his claws, Verminion's sheer size and impenetrable armor make him an astonishingly difficult foe – but this Named Lord's weapons aren't just physical. He is also known to be an incredibly "smooth talker", with the ability to seduce humans into doing things clearly not in their best interests (hence the nickname "The Deceiver"). More detail on this can be found in the previously referenced section on pg. 212, "The Unfortunate Case of (*name removed*) and the portalling of Verminion".

Weaknesses:
None discovered.

Final Thoughts:
There are no tactics offered for a confrontation with Verminion, because it is widely acknowledged that any confrontation will quickly result in your death. Only one person has ever been known to survive a direct face-to-face encounter with this Lord of the Nether but, given the tragic results, (*name removed*) probably wishes otherwise.

Be wary.

BARAKKAS

Hardly ever glimpsed, Barakkas has (thankfully) not yet been able to find a way to escape from the Nether and come to Earth. He resides in his black palace in the Inner Circle where he commands a horde of Class 5 monsters.

Only one human being has ever survived an encounter with Barakkas, and that person only survived for seven minutes. When (*name removed*) foolishly portalled into the Inner Circle on what he called a "scouting expedition", he never expected to come face-to-face with one of the Lords. Little is known about this encounter, because when (*name removed*) was rescued from the Nether, Nightmare Division agents were only able to recover his top half – Barakkas had apparently eaten the rest.

(*Name removed*) was able to provide scant few details about his attacker before he expired. What little information he was able to give us has been summarised below.

Description:
Three to five stories tall, Barakkas has leathery, cobalt-blue skin with enormous horns above his "Tyrannosaurus Rex-like" head, hooves that spark flame when striking the floor and eyes that change color depending on his mood. His mood is known to shift quickly and dramatically, hence the nickname "Barakkas The Rager". He can seem calm and charming, even friendly, before suddenly erupting into a rage and doing horrible things, like eating your legs.

Class:
Like all Named Lords, Barakkas is not ranked by Class number. He is unique.

Combat Tactics:
While very few humans have ever seen Barakkas in action, it is assumed that he uses his sheer size and speed to great advantage. His enormous jaw and shark-like teeth are capable of inflicting enormous damage (like eating legs) and his gigantic talons are no laughing matter, either.

Weaknesses:
None discovered.

Final Thoughts:
Like all the Named Lords, Barakkas is clearly desperate to come to Earth. If you mistakenly portal into his presence, it is best that you die quickly and honorably, thereby causing your portal to vanish and removing the only means he has to escape from the Nether and come to our world. Remember, only YOU can prevent Barakkas from raging across our planet!

SLAGGURON
Nothing known.

TYRANNUS
Nothing known.